LISA SUZANNE

ON DECK
VEGAS HEAT: BASES LOADED
BOOK THREE
© LISA SUZANNE 2024

All rights reserved. In accordance with the US Copyright Act of 1976, the scanning, uploading, and sharing of any part of this book without the permission of the publisher or author constitute unlawful piracy and theft of the author's intellectual property. No part of this book may be reproduced or transmitted in any form or by any means, electronic or mechanical, including photocopying, recording, or by any information storage and retrieval system without the written permission of the author, except where permitted by law and except for excerpts used in reviews. If you would like to use any words from this book other than for review purposes, prior written permission must be obtained from the publisher.

Published in the United States of America by Books by LS, LLC.

ISBN: 9798883884572

This book is a work of fiction. Any similarities to real people, living or dead, is purely coincidental. All characters and events in this work are figments of the author's imagination.

Books by Lisa Suzanne

VEGAS HEAT: THE EXPANSION TEAM
Curveball (Book One)
Fastball (Book Two)
Flyball (Book Three)
Groundball (Book Four)
Hardball (Book Five)

VEGAS ACES
Home Game (Book One)
Long Game (Book Two)
Fair Game (Book Three)
Waiting Game (Book Four)
End Game (Book Five)

VEGAS ACES: THE QUARTERBACK
Traded (Book One)
Tackled (Book Two)
Timeout (Book Three)
Turnover (Book Four)
Touchdown (Book Five)

VEGAS ACES: THE TIGHT END
Tight Spot (Book One)
Tight Hold (Book Two)
Tight Fit (Book Three)
Tight Laced (Book Four)
Tight End (Book Five)

VEGAS ACES: THE WIDE RECEIVER
Rookie Mistake (Book One)
Hidden Mistake (Book Two)
Honest Mistake (Book Three)
No Mistake (Book Four)
Favorite Mistake (Book Five)

Visit Lisa on Amazon for more titles

Dedication

To my favorite three.

Chapter 1
Alexis

I turn my phone back on with shaking fingers as I wonder whether Thanksgiving will always be clouded by this event moving forward.

Will I sit at the table next year with my father? Or will his seat be empty?

I'm not sitting at the table with him this year, and it's because I'm lying to him as I do things behind his back.

I didn't even call him to bid him a Happy Thanksgiving. I didn't call him to tell him how thankful I am for everything he's done for me.

I didn't call him because I'm hiding out with my boyfriend.

And now I might not get the chance to tell him everything I need to say.

Thank you for being there for me when we both lost Mom.

Thank you for raising me into the woman I am today.

I may be twenty-eight, but I still need my daddy.

I thought I was living the past twenty-four hours in complete bliss, but that bliss has quickly shifted into a nightmare.

I can't lose him.

I can't have *no* parents left. I'm too young. He's too young. So was my mother.

These details plague me as I wait for answers.

I have no idea what's going on, and Gregory found out exactly zero details, so I need to call Brooks. And if my father finds out where I am, well, so be it.

I need to know he's okay.

I ran upstairs immediately after telling Gregory *let's go* and I started throwing all my belongings back into my suitcase.

He has to be okay.

He's going to be okay.

I'm still throwing stuff while cradling my phone between my ear and shoulder when Brooks answers.

"Hello."

"Is he okay? What happened?" I demand. I pause what I'm doing to hold the phone tightly, as if that'll make the reply any different. Any better.

"He passed out during dinner. Just slumped over. Scared the hell out of my dad and me, so we called nine-one-one. The paramedics said he had low oxygen, but they won't tell me anything here at the hospital since I'm not immediate family."

"I'm coming home."

"When do you need to be back on set?" he asks.

"Monday, but if I don't make it, I don't make it."

He wouldn't want that. He wouldn't want me to put anything career-related on hold for him. But I will. I don't care if it costs thousands of dollars a day. I'll pay the difference—it's only money.

This is my dad we're talking about.

On Deck

Danny walks into the room just as I say the words. He watches me quietly while I pack and talk on the phone, and he walks over to his closet and grabs a small suitcase.

My heart lifts.

Is he coming, too?

No. He can't come. Obviously.

But I need him there. I need him to stand by my side while I walk into the unknown. I need him holding my hand as I hear whatever news awaits me.

"You don't have to. I can handle things here," he says.

"I need to see my father," I say flatly. I need to know for myself that he's going to be okay, but I don't feel like explaining that to Brooks. "I'll text flight details and keep messenger on. Let me know the second you hear anything."

We say our goodbyes, and I hang up and slide my phone into my pocket.

Danny clears his throat. "I booked you a flight. You and Gregory. It leaves in an hour, so it might be better to leave your stuff here and just take what you need for the next couple of days in this smaller suitcase since you have to be back here on Monday. I'll drive you to the airport and take care of the rental car and the Yukon."

My knees nearly give out at his words, at this show of *support* that I'm so not used to.

I have loyalty all around me. I have a huge fan base who adores every move I make. I have legions of people who know every word to every song, those who read into the lyrics and search for cryptic clues. I have people who solve puzzles I didn't even intend to make.

But I don't have any normal relationships, including with my own father. Including my manager.

I'm locked in a prison in my own home, and the sting of loneliness grates on me sometimes.

Or it did, anyway. Until Danny.

Now *he* feels like home. He's the very definition of home—a place of belonging where I'm safe and loved and can be my true, authentic self.

And I'm leaving this home we've built over the last few months to head back to the prison.

He sees I'm about to fall, and he swoops in to hold me up, grabbing me into his arms and holding me tightly.

"I wish you could come," I say, and I'm not sure I've ever needed someone as much as I need him right now. I need his hand in mine. I need him here by my side telling me how everything is going to be okay.

It will be okay…right?

This is my father we're talking about. Sure, we've had some disagreements about my career, but every family has disagreements. Most don't work together the way we do. He's still the man who captured my first steps on video, the man who warned off the boy who took me to my freshman year homecoming dance, the man whose hand I held at my mother's funeral. He's still my dad despite the arguments we've had over the last few months.

And at the center of those arguments is *me*. I'm the one changing and growing while he's been stuck in the way we've done things for the last twelve years. He's comfortable there, and we've had a lot of success together—which is why it's hard to make a change.

I can't help but wonder if the blame for whatever this health crisis is falls on my shoulders.

Did the stress of his daughter wanting to stop working with him cause some kind of issue?

Danny holds me for a few beats while all this darts through my mind. I hold tightly to him as the conflicting thoughts swirl around me. The only thing I'm sure of right now is my feelings for the man holding me.

"I'm not ready to leave, but I have to," I whisper. I can't make my voice work because now I'm crying.

He squeezes me tighter, and he drops a kiss on my cheek. "It'll be okay, Lex. I'm right here for anything you need."

"I know. And I love you."

"I love you," he says back to me, and his lips catch mine for a quick kiss that's far too short.

He zips up the small suitcase, and Gregory is already waiting downstairs by the front door. Danny's mom is standing near him, and she reaches out to pull me into a hug.

"My sweet girl. You check in with us when you get home, okay? It's been the greatest pleasure in the world seeing you with my boy the last twenty-four hours, and I can't wait until I get to see you again," she says, only prompting the tears to fall harder.

I cling to her tightly for a beat, and the feeling is overwhelming as I realize it's been eighteen years since a mother figure has hugged me this way.

"Thank you, Tracy," I say softly.

Anna hugs me next. "We'll miss you. Safe travels, and let us know when you've arrived, okay?"

I feel like we're all avoiding the words *Happy Thanksgiving*. It doesn't feel so happy right now since I have to leave this wonderful family to get back home to my own.

"Thank you all for such a wonderful day. I'm thankful I got to spend the holiday with you." Even though I feel guilty that I wasn't there celebrating it with my father.

Maybe that's why I feel pressed to get back home to him. I should've been there, and the fact that I wasn't makes me feel like a bad daughter.

Lying, sneaking around…this isn't me. Or it wasn't, anyway. Until I met Danny.

And that's all my father will see if I tell him the truth.

If I even get that chance.

I hug everyone one last time, saving Danny for last.

He holds me a moment longer than is necessary, and I know I'll call up the memory of this embrace in my hours of loneliness to come.

He kisses me softly, and then we head out to the car. We sit in the backseat together, and he tosses an arm around me and pulls me into his chest. He holds my hand, and we're quiet back here as Gregory navigates toward the airport.

We head toward a private entrance where Gregory cuts the engine. Danny and I share one last kiss, and he leans his forehead to mine. "I love you, Lex. I'm here for whatever you need."

Tears brim in my eyes. I can't physically make myself say goodbye as I force myself out of the car and into the building without looking back.

Because I'm afraid if I look back, I won't go. I'll stay here with Danny in this place that suddenly feels like the warmest, most inviting home I've ever been to.

But my father needs me.

Chapter 2
Danny

I went unrecognized in large thanks to the fact that we used the private entrance that I'm quite familiar with at this point, but also because I had a hoodie on and there really wasn't anybody around when I slipped out of the back seat and into the front.

I drive away as if I'm not leaving an entire piece of myself in her hands.

I'm worried about her. It's silly, I know. She's an adult woman, but she's scared because of whatever it is her father is going through, and I can't be there with her by her side to help her navigate it.

I've never cared about navigating something with someone else.

There are so many firsts with her that I've started to lose count. But the most important first is the fact that I've fallen in love with her.

I want to be where she is.

That's not possible—this I know. I dedicated my life to baseball long before I met her, just as she dedicated hers to her own talents. We have completely separate lives in completely separate spheres, and while part of that is a *good* thing since we have our own likes and interests, that doesn't make it any easier when we're forced apart—whatever the reason.

All I know is that I don't want to spend another second without her…and I just said goodbye to her at the airport.

It's not fair that I can't be by her side to hold her hand as the nerves of waiting rack her during the short flight back to LA.

It's not fair that I can't walk into her father's hospital room with her, that I can't be there by her side to comfort her for whatever news she's about to face.

And I don't blame her for going to him. Perhaps they have a difference of opinion when it comes to her career, but he's her only surviving parent. She *should* be there, just as I'd be there for my mother if the roles were reversed.

But knowing she's suffering, crippled with fear because she has no idea what she's walking into, and I can't be there for her…it's a tough form of suffering in my own right, too.

I head home in the rental car that I'll drop off sometime tomorrow, and when I get there, the house is quiet.

"Where is everybody?" I ask my mother when I find her on my couch reading a book.

"Anna and Rush are upstairs reading bedtime books to the boys. You okay?"

"Anna *and Rush*?" I repeat. Part of me wants him to go. Part of me wants this just to be family. But part of me wonders whether he *will* become a part of this family, and I don't really hate that thought as much as I thought I would. "Good for those two. And yeah…I'm okay."

On Deck

"Come here," she says, holding her arms open as she sets the book down, and I sit beside her on the couch and rest my head on her shoulder.

She leans over and presses an awkward kiss to the top of my head. "I can tell how much you like her, Danny. I'm really happy for you."

"It's more than like, Mom."

"I know, honey. And it's clear she feels the same for you."

"You really think so?"

"I know so." She pats my leg. "And she's...well, she's perfect for you. She's kind and silly and fun. She's smart and so, so talented. She's sweet and seems like she keeps herself out of trouble."

"She does." Except for, you know, getting high with me the other night, a fact which I omit to my mother despite being two years from thirty. "And she is all those things." I love how she didn't call on her beauty first. At all, actually. Anyone can see she's a gorgeous girl, but it's what's inside that I've fallen for.

Head over fucking feet.

Or whatever the phrase is.

"What about you and Magnum PI?" I ask as I sit up. I glance over at her, and her brows are knit together.

"Who?"

"Gregory."

I swear I see a tinge of pink color her cheeks.

"What about him? He seems like a nice man who has a very important job that he takes quite seriously."

"I don't know if anyone has ever called him a *nice man* before," I tease.

"Well, he was nice to me."

"How nice are we talking?" I ask, wiggling my eyebrows suggestively.

"Daniel James!" she scolds, picking up the pillow next to her and hitting me with it in the chest.

"Hey, I'm just looking out for my mama," I protest with a laugh.

"Well your mama appreciates that, but really, it was nothing. Just one little kiss—" She cuts herself off as her eyes widen, and she slaps a hand over her mouth.

"Mother! What did you just say?" My own eyes widen as I sit up straighter.

"I'm totally teasing you, Danny. But you should've seen your reaction just then. Quite comical." She laughs at her own joke.

I shoot her a glare. "That wasn't very nice."

"Neither is teasing your mother about your girlfriend's good-looking bodyguard." She lifts a shoulder.

"Fine. My deepest apologies. But really, have you ever, you know...thought about dating?"

"I *have* dated, honey. But the pool isn't quite as full when you get to a certain age, and there aren't a whole lot of options open. And your girlfriend's bodyguard? I wouldn't want to get involved with someone who's involved with someone close to you. It's too messy. Too complicated. And besides, he's lost a lot in his life, and I don't even know that he's interested in getting back into things."

"All I really heard you say just then is that you're interested and you want me to find out for you."

She yanks the pillow she threw at me out of my arms where I'm clutching it and smacks me with it again. "Don't you dare," she hisses.

I laugh, and I'm still laughing when Rush and Anna come down the stairs without the boys.

"The boys asleep?" my mom asks, and Anna nods.

My mom heads up to bed, and Anna goes up to her room for a while to check some emails related to projects back home, giving Rush and me a few minutes alone.

"Beer?" I ask, and he nods.

We each crack one open and head out to my patio, where we slide into chairs and tap cans in a toast to nothing other than drinking a beer.

"You okay, man?" he asks.

I nod. "As okay as I can be given the strangeness of it all. The secrets, the lying, not being able to be there for her."

He presses his lips together as he nods. "Listen, as someone who knows what it's like to keep a secret and be stuck in one place when you want to be somewhere else, I feel you."

His words finally sink in, and I can't help but wonder for the first time if it was *me* who kept him away from my sister. They got to know each other in secret without telling me, and now he's having Thanksgiving dinner with us.

In all honesty, I feel like shit that I'm the one who kept them apart. Nobody has the right to do that to anybody else even though I did it unknowingly since it was their choice not to tell me.

Seven or eight months ago, would I have had a different reaction? Would I have told him he couldn't be with her? Am I more understanding now because of Alexis?

Abso-fucking-lutely.

"Look, man. I'm sorry if I had a part in you two running around in secret even if I didn't know I did. I'm sorry you kept shit from me. You shouldn't have had to do that, and I promise to make things right," I say.

He shrugs and shakes his head. "Water under the bridge. But if you really want to make things right, then don't say no to what I want to ask you." He tips his can to his lips.

My brows dip. "What do you want to ask me?"

He clears his throat, and his eyes dart around my yard before they land back on me. "I love your sister, man. I'm falling in love with those two little boys, too. She's thinking about moving here to Vegas so we can give this a real shot."

"Oh Jesus. I thought you were going to ask me for her hand in marriage," I say.

He laughs. "Dude, we've only been seeing each other a few months. Her divorce isn't final yet, and talk of marriage hasn't entered the equation. I don't even know if she wants that again for herself, anyway."

"Do *you* want that?" I ask.

He lifts a shoulder. "More now than I ever did in the past. You?"

"Same. Actually…" I trail off. I haven't told anybody what I've been thinking, and maybe it'll help to talk it out before I make any major moves.

"Actually…what?" he presses.

"Her dad wants her to go through with the wedding to Brooks. I got to thinking, what if I married her first? Then she couldn't do it." I chug the rest of my beer after the words leave my mouth.

His brows shoot up. "You serious, man?"

I nod. "Dead serious. I discovered there are confidential marriage licenses available in California to keep it fully secret. Other states have them, too. So we could quietly get married, and then she wouldn't be able to marry Brooks."

"Wow, you even did research? So you really *are* serious. Would she agree to it?"

I press my lips together. "I don't know. I haven't brought it up to her, but I know things with her father were already tense, and now this health scare…who knows how it's going to affect things."

On Deck

As it turns out, it affects far more than I ever imagined it would.

Chapter 3
Alexis

I've been wringing my hands in my lap for the last hour, and I haven't heard from Brooks at all. Not a single word to let me know my dad is doing okay or any sort of update. Nothing.

I tried listening to music as that's my usual distraction, but it did nothing for me today.

Instead, I feel lost as I stare out the tiny airplane window with a baseball hat on in some futile attempt to avoid being recognized.

The problem today is that *Gregory* was recognized, and as much as he tried to shield me, people saw me, too.

I signed autographs. I smiled.

Nobody cares that I'm dealing with a family emergency. Nobody has any idea what's clawing inside of me. They only see one side of it, so if I'm not perfectly polite and they have a bad experience, that reflects on how they feel about my music.

It doesn't matter that I'm fighting emotions and inner turmoil and fear over what's going on with my father. If I don't stop and give whoever's asking me for an autograph a moment of my time, I look like the ungrateful bitch who doesn't care about her fans when nothing could be further from the truth. I love them, and I'm grateful for them every single day. I wouldn't be able to do this without them.

They don't know that my father is in the hospital. They don't know that I don't know the reason why and I'm scared as I wait for word about what's going on. They don't know that I'm faking my engagement with Brooks and I'm in love with Danny Brewer. They don't know that I would rather be with Danny right now, holding his hand through these tense moments. They don't know anything about me personally other than what my father allows them to see.

It's for my own protection and privacy, which I can appreciate, but this thing I'm feeling with Danny makes me want to shout from the rooftops about what I've found with him.

Not being allowed to do that because it'll make me look a certain way or make Danny look a certain way feels like the biggest betrayal to my fans. To the world. To him and me.

But these are things I can't dwell on right now. Instead, I'm choosing to focus on the many blessings I do have.

So rather than tell Katie at the airport that I don't want to take a selfie, or rather than tell Tiffany as she hands me a piece of paper to sign that I don't want to do those things right now, I grin and bear it.

As more people recognize me while Gregory tries to usher me through the airport and the paparazzi start snapping photos upon our arrival at LAX, I realize what a strange life I lead.

While I'm certainly one of the lucky few, I don't get to just walk through an airport to get to my car.

Sometimes I think about running away from it all.

I've never honestly considered that. I have too many responsibilities, places to be, and things to do. But what if?

What if I did just run away from it all and ran straight into Danny's arms?

Even better, what if Danny ran away with me?

What if we were able to go somewhere where nobody could find us, and I even escaped Gregory and my father and Brooks, and I just…ran?

What if we could have that time together when nobody knew who we were and nobody cared, and we were just another couple walking down the street in the sunlight?

The pressures of this business are overwhelming, and they're even stronger and harder to deal with when you add in the fear over what's going on with my father.

Will he be okay? I still don't know. I still haven't heard from Brooks. I still don't know what's going on.

What would my dad think if he knew I was at Danny's Thanksgiving dinner table, laughing with his mother and bonding with his sister over our shared disgust of green bean casserole?

What if I just told him? What if I stopped hiding and told him the truth about how I've fallen in love with a baseball player?

Somehow, I don't think it would matter. Because, as much as I love my father, he has his own agenda, and he's not going to stop until he gets what he wants. And what he wants is a merger with D3 Management.

Why?

I don't know.

Maybe in some bid to take over the world.

All I know is that he has to be okay…and I send up a silent wish that I will do anything for him to be okay.

Be careful what you wish for.

We finally arrive at the hospital, and I'm ushered straight back. I bypass the ER waiting room completely, instead going into the ambulance entrance for my own privacy, so I don't even see Brooks.

My father is awake and appears...well, fine—mostly. He's got an oxygen tube under his nose, his only sign of distress apart from some coughing, and he's barking at the poor nurse when I peek my head in. "Alexis! What are you doing here?"

Immediate relief floods me.

"Happy Thanksgiving, Daddy," I say softly. "Are you okay?"

"I'm fine. Fine! I've been taking that medicine for my knee, and they're telling me it's some immunosuppressant or something. I guess that means I got really sick but didn't know I was really sick."

"It means pulmonary edema," the nurse says, raising her brows and looking at him pointedly.

"That sounds serious," I say.

"Pneumonia," he clarifies, looking at me. "I passed out from low oxygen. I'm fine now."

"He will be fine, but I can't say that the oral antibiotic he'll be prescribed will make him any nicer," the nurse teases, and I can't help a giggle at that.

"Can you work on that before you release him?" I beg, and the nurse shoots me a smile before she walks out of the room.

"You didn't have to come all this way, Alexis," he scolds.

"It's okay, Dad. I wanted to. I needed to see you, and they wouldn't tell Brooks anything."

"Well, I'm fine," he snaps.

"That's good. And I can be here for the next few days before I head back to Vegas for the location shoot."

"I'd like that," he says, patting my hand as he leans back. "Except they gave me something that makes me have to pee, and I have to go again. Go out in the hall for a minute, would you?"

I laugh as I walk outside, and relief floods me. He calls me back in, and we chat for a while.

"How was your turkey dinner?" I ask, knowing it was catered from the same place he orders from every year.

"Fine until I ruined a perfectly good plate of mashed potatoes and gravy by passing out in it," he says, and I swear there's a twinkle in his eye.

I wrinkle my nose. "Dad! Did that really happen?"

"Brooks and Arthur were worried I was going to snort up the potatoes." He rolls his eyes and shakes his head a little. "No, that's not what really happened. I kind of just slumped backward into my seat."

"How terrifying," I murmur.

"I didn't even know what was going on, so it wasn't so bad for me. Until I came to, and they were carting me onto an ambulance." He shrugs.

"You're quite the jokester today," I say.

"Defense mechanism," he admits.

He does that a lot over the next couple days, because as it turns out, he has a bit of a stay before he's released from the hospital. They're keeping an eye on his lung functions, and he's been irritable and coughing, but as we progress through the days, he heals up just fine as I spend time by his side, making sure he's doing everything his nurses tell him to do—none of which he *wants* to do because he's stubborn as a mule, but I do my best to step in as the voice of reason. I tell him I need him here with me, so he needs to do what they say.

Usually that's enough to spur him into better behavior.

Not always, but usually.

Little do I know what he's planning under the mask of good behavior.

Chapter 4
Alexis

He's released on Sunday evening, and I already booked the first flight back to Vegas for tomorrow morning so I make sure to arrive on time for my first day on set. It won't give me time to see Danny in the morning, but at least I'll be back at work.

Gregory drives us all home. Brooks is in the front passenger seat, and I'm in the back with my dad. I reach over and squeeze his hand.

"You can't leave me yet, Daddy," I say softly. "I need you taking care of yourself."

I know we're both thinking the same thing. We lost my mom far too young, and he's the only parent I have left. Life is short, and over the last nearly twenty years since she's been gone, there were many times we only had each other to lean on.

I have Danny now, though my dad doesn't know that. Danny has been nothing short of completely amazing since all this happened. He's been checking in on me, calling me, and sending donuts and bacon and flowers to the house through Gregory.

I lied and told my dad the flowers were for him.

But I didn't share the bacon.

I feel a huge sense of relief that my dad is back home now, though worry still plagues me. I know I lost my mom years and years ago, and it should've given me this sense that my father won't live forever, but it didn't. We never think they'll leave us until they're gone.

All this situation is doing is making me see how short life is.

It's making me see how important my father is to me. He's been there through every major milestone in my life—personally and professionally–and he's the only person in the world who hasn't wavered. My high school friends wavered. They didn't understand what I was doing. They didn't know what the future held, and back then, it was easier just to let go of friendships. They were jealous, and I didn't have the power to make them feel any other way.

I'd love to get closer with Reese—the lead singer of Vail's wife. She's always been so friendly to me, and she understands what this life is like.

Or maybe even Anna—Danny's sister. She's got a famous brother, and never once in the short amount of time I just spent with her did I feel like she wanted my money or my fame. She's just a down to earth, sweet lady doing her best with her kids as she explores this thing with her brother's best friend.

But those thoughts are put on hold as I head down to my dad's office to tell him goodnight.

"Shouldn't you be resting?" I ask as I walk in.

"I'm fine," he says, a touch of petulance in his voice.

"You just got out of the hospital, Dad. They told you to take it easy."

He gives me a pointed look then nods to the chair across from his desk—his silent way of telling me to sit. I do.

"Are you doing okay with all this?" he asks.

I shrug. "As okay as I can be. I don't exactly want to leave tomorrow to go film a movie when I know you're not going to take orders from anyone other than me, and I want to make sure you're healing and happy."

He rolls his eyes.

"Just please take your medicine," I beg. "Okay?"

"Yeah, yeah."

"Dad," I say firmly, and he glances up at me. "We already lost Mom, okay? I can't lose you too. Life is short, and I need you here with me."

"I know it's short," he mutters. "All too well." He folds his arms across his chest and leans back in his chair. "Which is why I want to be sure you're taken care of."

"I *am* taken care of," I say, thinking of how Danny really did take care of me over the last few days even from a distance. "I promise. I'm happy."

"Since you just said you want to make sure I'm healing and happy…I want you to consider doing something that will bring me joy."

My brows dip. "Like what?"

"Go through with the wedding…and sooner than I first said. If you're really worried about me and my health, I feel like *this* is the thing that will give me the comfort I need. We need to get this thing wrapped up."

Jeez. Talk about controlling me with fear combined with obligation.

"Really, Dad? Me marrying Brooks is what will give you the comfort you need after a bout of pneumonia?" I ask.

I don't need to wait for his answer. I already know what it is.

I'm not sure why he's so desperate for this, but he's right about one thing.

I just said I want him to be happy.

And if this is the thing that'll make him happy…what choice do I have?

"Please, Alexis. Just do this one thing for me. It'll take a whole lot of stress off me to get this merger to go through, and marriage is the next phase of your brand development anyway."

It can be temporary. It can be for show. It can be for the brand.

It sure as hell won't be for me.

I stare at him for a long time, not sure what to say.

He keeps talking before I get a chance to. "Then after the wedding, we can discuss who you'd like representing you as your agent. Perhaps someone from D3 once the merger goes through, or maybe someone at Bodega. It'll be your choice."

My choice.

Nothing about any of this feels like *my choice*.

It's a terrible idea. I don't want to do it.

But this whole health scare could've been a lot worse. I could've lost him. We got lucky that I didn't, but it sort of feels like we're on borrowed time now.

Is it really that big a deal to go through with this for him, for the media, for the merger?

It'll give me what I want in the end—control over my own career.

And with that in mind, the word slips out before I can stop it.

"Okay."

I regret it the second I say it, but it feels like there's no turning back now.

Chapter 5
Danny

I don't shoot until tomorrow, but I decide to swing by the set today anyway since I know Alexis is back in town. Gregory took her from the airport directly to the studio, and I figured it wouldn't hurt to pretend like I just stopped by to check shit out when the truth is I'd love to find her trailer and hang there when she's between scenes…or however all this works.

I easily find her trailer once I get past security since it's marked with *A. Bodega*, and I glance around and find myself alone. I walk up the three steps and knock quietly on the door, and it opens a beat later.

She stands there in all her perfect glory, and she yanks me inside. She slams the door behind me, pushes up onto her tiptoes, and meets my lips with hers. I sling an arm around her waist and haul her in close, and she jumps up and links her legs around my waist as she cups my jaw between her hands.

"God, I missed you," I breathe against her lips, and she opens her mouth to mine as our tongues batter together.

She pulls back and looks into my eyes, and I see something there.

Something I haven't seen before—not when she's looking at me, anyway.

I can't quite identify what it is, but it's something along the lines of fear.

"What's wrong?" I ask immediately.

"How do you know something's wrong?"

"It's all over your face, Lex. You can't hide from me."

She lets out a sigh and drops her legs, but I don't let her out of my arms.

"What's going on?" My voice is full of the alarm I feel pulsing through my chest.

She clears her throat. "I, uh…my dad—well…" She's stuttering, and this nervous girl isn't the confident woman I've come to know.

"It's okay, Lex. Whatever it is." I press my lips to her forehead to give her the comfort I know she needs.

She bursts into tears, pulls back from me, and starts fanning her eyes. "Shit. My make-up. They already did it, and I can't mess it up. I have to go to the studio soon."

"What's going on?"

She sniffles as she tries to regain her composure, and her eyes dart around the room before landing back on me. "My dad…it was scary. The whole thing was scary. And he's the only family I have left, so I have to do what's right, and, well, that's…"

"You're scaring me, Lex," I say quietly.

"I told him I'd marry Brooks."

"You what?" I breathe, sure I heard her wrong.

She closes her eyes and nods. "I have to. It's for him. He said it would make him so happy to know I'm taken care of—"

"But *I* can take care of you!" I roar.

"I know that, and you know that, but he doesn't. He trusts Brooks and says it's for the brand and the merger, and I need to just do this one thing." She sounds so unsure of herself, and I *know* this isn't the Alexis I've fallen in love with.

She went to California for a few nights, and somehow, they sent back the wrong person.

"Don't marry him." I'm begging, but I don't know what else to do.

"I have to. It's for my father." She sniffles, then steps away from me, further out of my grasp, to grab a tissue. She wraps it around her finger to blot the inside of her eyes. "He's the only family I have left."

"It's emotional blackmail, Alexis. For him to even *ask* you is emotional blackmail."

She nods. "I know it is. It's about control. It's about playing on my obligations and fears and guilt. But the *why* doesn't matter. The fact is that I agreed to do it."

Marry me instead.

I'm tempted to say the words but can't quite get them out. I can't make this harder on her than it already is, not when she's hurting and scared.

My role here is to take care of her, and I will do that in whatever way I can. But I'm terrified I won't be able to do it for much longer—not if she's married to another man.

Have I been a fool all along? Does she even love me?

When my eyes meet hers, I have to believe she does.

Still, this hurts. It stabs a knife right into my guts, twisting and turning until I can no longer bear the pain.

"How long?" I ask quietly.

Her brows dip. "Until the wedding?"

I lift a shoulder. "Yeah. Until the wedding, but also...how long did you agree to stay married?"

"We didn't get into the finer details," she admits. "He originally said January, but after this whole health scare, he said he wants to move it sooner."

"And for how long?"

She shrugs. "I won't stay with him longer than a year. My dad told me as soon as my last name is Donovan, he'll sign over my contract to another agent. So as soon as the merger is finalized, I imagine the divorce will be next."

I walk over and pull her back into my arms because it's my instinct. It's what I have to do to try to lessen the pain screaming through me. "I hate this, Alexis."

"I know. I do, too. Believe me. But I don't have a choice." She's getting emotional again, and I don't want to make things worse even though I think this is the worst idea in the history of terrible ideas.

Ask her to marry you.

The voice in my head is pulsing at me, but I can't bring myself to do it. Not yet. She's here for the next week with me.

We can make this work.

I have time.

It's short and limited, but I have *some*, and that's what I have to bank on right now.

I blow out a breath as I try to dredge up the courage to say what I need to say, but a knock at the door stops me.

She glances at me and then at the door, and I move back behind the door as she pulls it open.

"You're needed on set, Ms. Bodega," a female voice announces.

"Thank you," she says. "I'll be right there."

She closes the door, and I'm still standing there right behind it.

On Deck

The pain in her eyes slices through me as she says, "I'm sorry, Danny. I understand if it's not right for you to hang around waiting for me."

I reach over and haul her back into me. "I will wait forever for you if I need to."

She tips her head back, and I lean down to kiss her.

I just pray there are many more of these kisses to come and that we aren't staring down at the inevitable end.

Chapter 6
Alexis

The way I see it, we have two options.

We can lean on each other for support, or we can let this tear us apart.

I know Danny has trust issues, and I don't blame him after the things he's been through—the things he's seen.

But I also get the very real sense that he not only understands why I have to do this, but he trusts me because he believes in us.

And I like to think I had a part in helping him believe in love the way he does now.

This thing with Brooks won't last forever. Soon enough, we will figure out how we can move forward.

And so, after I'm done with my scene and return to my very own trailer, I'm thrilled beyond measure that Danny is sitting there on my couch waiting for me.

"Where are you staying?" he demands when I walk in.

"They're putting us up at the Wynn."

"You're staying with me."

I nod, as if there was ever a question. "I'll let Gregory know."

"He can stay at the Wynn. I'll drop you off in the morning, and he can get you back to set."

I laugh. We both know why he wants me with him and Gregory elsewhere, and I have exactly zero complaints about that.

I'm just glad he's not running the other way. He could. Maybe he *should*, even. But I'm grateful he isn't. I'm grateful he trusts in what we have enough to stick this out with me…whatever that might mean going forward.

I pull my phone out of my pocket and text Gregory. He's on call while I'm on set all day since the film has its own security, and I'm done filming for the day, anyway.

"Ms. Bodega?" he answers.

"Hi Gregory. Danny is here with me, and he's taking me back to his place tonight, so you can have the night off, okay?"

"Ma'am," he says, and he inflects the end almost like a question. We've been together long enough that I know what he's asking.

I hand the phone to Danny. "He'd like a word with you."

"Hello?" Danny says after holding the phone up to his ear.

I don't hear what Gregory says, but I hear Danny's side of the conversation: "No, I don't…yes, that would be fine…sure…okay, we'll see you soon."

"See you soon?" I ask as he ends the call. He hands the phone back to me.

"He made a good point that I wouldn't be able to sneak you out to the car without getting caught, so he's on his way to pick you up here. He'll drop you at my house."

I roll my eyes even though it's probably better this way.

He pauses a beat like he wants to say something but then seems to let it go. "I'll head out first, okay? I'll see you over there."

I squint at him and set a hand on my hip. "What were you going to say?"

He sighs, presses his lips together, and shakes his head a little. "I hate hiding, Lex, and I keep thinking it's *all* we're going to be doing. It's not right."

"I know it's not, and I'm sorry. I just…I guess I don't see another way out."

He studies me for a few beats, and then he nods. "Find out what your dad is thinking first, okay? If he's got a date in mind. Then we'll figure something out."

I nod. "Okay. I'll talk to him tonight."

"You don't have to rush it. Wait until you're back home."

I consider his advice, but I already know I've made up my mind, and there's little he can do to change it.

And that's why as soon as I'm tucked safely in the back of the SUV Gregory is driving around Vegas this week, I dial up my father.

"How was the first day of filming on location in Vegas?" he answers.

"Great. I'm really finding my groove with the rest of the cast, and it feels like I was made to play this part," I tell him.

"Wonderful."

"How are you feeling?" I ask a little cautiously.

"Fine, fine."

"Did you take your medicine today?" I press.

"Yes, my dear. I did. Now lay off your old man, will you?"

"Sorry, sorry. Listen, Dad, I need to ask you something," I begin. I force my acting hat on and pretend like I'm not terrified to have this conversation.

"What is it?"

"Are you still thinking January for the wedding?" I rush the words before I can stop myself.

"Oh, honey, I don't want you to worry about that. You just get through your location shoot and get back home to Los Angeles, and then we'll talk about it."

Something about the way he says it makes me uncomfortable…as if he's keeping something from me. I decide to call him on it. "What aren't you telling me?"

He sighs. "I wanted to wait and surprise you when you got back. I was able to move up the date at San Ysidro instead of the Peninsula, and I talked with Brian about your schedule. You're off the fifteenth, and San Ysidro shifted another party to accommodate you, and, well…"

"The fifteenth?" I repeat.

"Yes."

"Of December?"

"Yes."

"As in…" I count quickly in my head. "As in nineteen *days?*"

"As in nineteen days," he confirms.

"Dad, you can't pull off a wedding in nineteen days." I'm trying to be logical here, but clearly logic has flown the coop.

"Watch me," he says a little thickly.

I guess the shorter the timeframe, the less people will know. But this doesn't seem like an event he *doesn't* want everyone to know about. I'm sure he's already sold the exclusive first photos to *People Magazine* or whoever the highest bidder will be. I'm sure he's already tipped off the paparazzi.

My chest feels tight, like my racing heart is trying to burst out of it.

My throat feels too big for my neck, like I'm choking on something.

I'm panicking. I know I'm panicking. It's not my first panic attack, and I'm sure it won't be my last.

Breathe, Carrie. Breathe. I'm right here.

My mom's voice is faint, but it's still there even after two decades, giving me the same reminder she did many years ago.

She coached me through my first panic attack. I was eight, and my parents had gotten into a fight, and little eight-year-old Carrie was scared her parents were heading for divorce. They weren't—my parents loved each other very much, but as a kid, I neither knew nor appreciated that fact. I was just plain scared.

And that's all this is. I'm scared to marry Brooks. I'm scared I'm going to lose what I've built with Danny when he's the one I want to be with. I'm scared for my dad's health. I'm scared of what'll happen if I go through with the wedding. I'm scared of what'll happen if I don't.

Once again, I'm just plain scared.

Breathe, Carrie. Breathe. I'm right here.

I learned how to manage these episodes way back then.

Step one? Eliminate the trigger.

"I have to go." I hang up on my dad, apathetic to the consequences.

I lean my head back on the seat and close my eyes as I try to focus on my breathing.

Step two? Breathe.

"You okay, ma'am?" Gregory asks from up front.

"Fine," I lie.

Step three? Seek help.

I open my eyes and click call on the only contact I need right now.

"Lex?" Danny answers.

"My dad set a new date. The fifteenth." I hear the panic in my own tone.

"Of..." he asks, trailing off.

"Next month. December. Nineteen days."

"Fuck," he mutters. "Are you okay?"

"No." The word comes out as a sob.

"Jesus, Lex. I'm so sorry. We'll figure this out, okay? I promise. Whatever you have to do, you won't be alone. I'm right here."

I'm right here.

I start to cry outright as the three words stab right into my heart.

Of course he's here. He's dependable. He's incredible.

He's mine.

And because of him, I've never felt so safe in my entire life.

Chapter 7
Danny

I'm waiting by my front door when the Yukon pulls into my driveway. Gregory ushers her to my front door, and I grab her into my arms.

"I'll be by at six tomorrow for pick up," he says more to me than her since her face is smashed against my chest, and she's clinging to me like she hasn't seen me in years. "She has a make-up call at six-fifteen."

I hide my concern in front of Gregory for her sake. She's here now, and I wasn't lying when I said I was here for her.

"Thank you," I tell him, and he nods curtly before he turns to leave. He pauses, and he turns back.

"If you need anything…" he trails off.

"I know," I say quietly. "Thank you again."

He nods, and I get the very real sense that he trusts me. And something about knowing that the only person in her life who knows about *us* trusts me with her gives me everything I need to be whatever *she* needs in this moment.

I let her cling to me as I close the door behind him and flip the bolt. I hold onto her tightly and press a kiss to the top of her head.

"I'm right here," I say again, and I rub her back as she starts to cry. "Hey, baby, it's okay. If you don't want to marry him, you don't have to."

"I just feel so stuck," she wails. It's the same conversation we've already had. We're beating a dead horse here.

"I know. And if you need to go through with it, then you go through with it. It'll be okay. I'll be right here on the other side."

"I don't expect you to be," she says, her voice trembling through her tears. "I can't ask that of you. I don't know what other manipulations my dad will place on me. I don't know how long he expects this to last. I don't know anything about anything, and I can't force you to wait when the answers are all unknown."

"It doesn't matter to me." My words are backed with vehemence. "I said it once, and I'll say it again. I would wait forever for you."

She cries harder, and I hold her tighter.

It's the first time in my life I found someone worth waiting for. I'm not going to let this little hiccup with her father get in the way of our happy ending.

I believe in us. I believe that there *will* be a happy ending down the line for us.

I just have no idea what it'll take to get there.

While I was hoping for a *fun* night together, this is something else entirely.

But it's still exactly what we need. It's strengthening our bond and feeding us something we didn't know we were hungry for.

It's letting me show her that this isn't just about sex. It's about the friendship we built before we ever had sex. Sex is just the added bonus on top of the incredible relationship we've created.

On Deck

We don't stand by the front door all night. When she stops crying, I sweep her into my arms and carry her into the family room, where we sit together on the couch. She snuggles into my chest, and I hold her close with my arm around her shoulder.

"What happened?" I ask.

"Panic attack," she admits.

"You mentioned once before that mental health was something you wanted to advocate for. Have you had panic attacks before?" I ask softly.

She nods. "My first was when I was eight. My mom helped coach me through it. When I lost her, they got worse, and I guess the fear of losing my dad or upsetting him or whatever is triggering to me. I've learned how to manage them thanks to the help of a therapist, but sometimes they pop up. And the things you said…" She trails off as she shakes her head a little. "I can still hear my mom's voice. *Breathe, Carrie. Breathe. I'm right here.* You told me you were right here, and it somehow instantly brought me back and calmed me. It was like I knew everything would be okay because you were here."

I tighten my hold around her shoulder. "I *am* right here. Through this whole thing. Whatever it is. Whatever happens. However much it goes against everything I believe in when it comes to marriage…I'm here. Okay? And I'm not going anywhere."

She leans back to look up at me. "I love you."

"I love you, too." I drop my lips to hers, and it's a slow, sweet kiss that says everything we both need to say without the words.

Eventually I carry her up to bed, and I hold her against my body the whole night through. When the alarm rings at five, it wakes me from a deep sleep.

I usually sleep pretty well, but I think I sleep even better with her beside me than without.

I wish we could wake like this every morning. I wish a lot of things, but mostly, I just wish we could be like everybody else in love. That we could live free and clear of whatever rules her father put in place so long ago that she feels she still needs to abide by.

I'm trying to understand it all, but the more time I spend with her, the deeper I fall...the more I think she just needs to fucking stand up to him.

But how do I tell her that?

She's afraid for him. He was just in the hospital. She's scared one wrong move on her part will put him back there, and I can't blame her. She already lost her mother. He's the one parent she has left, and it must be terrifying for her to think about losing him, too—especially when they're as close as they are. She may not like everything he does, but since he's also her agent, his life and hers are even more inextricably tied than most fathers and daughters.

I gently shake her awake. "Lex, you wanted to wake up at five."

"Mm," she says softly. She shifts her ass back toward me, and as much as I want to give her space for whatever it is she needs...I *am* still a man.

And I'm definitely *up* for the challenge this morning. Or my cock is, anyway.

She moans when I shift my hips against her ass, and that's all the invitation I need. I reach under her shirt and start massaging her breast, and she goads me on with more of her moans. I pinch her nipple, and she offers more encouragement. I lower my hand down into her panties since she slept only in one of my t-shirts, and she groans when I cup her pussy with my hand. I part those sweet lips down below with two fingers, and I rub against her clit before driving both fingers into her.

On Deck

She pushes her hips down to meet my fingers drive for drive, and I reach under her with my other hand to massage those sweet tits while I finger fuck her. Her moans get louder as she gets closer, and I shove my dick against her ass as he begs to break free from the confines of my boxer briefs.

I was trying to be polite when we went to bed last night since she wasn't mentally in the place for sex. But this morning is clearly an entirely different story.

I press my lips to her neck as she arches back against me, and her moans are so fucking hot that I nearly lose it. I force myself to rein it in, still a little embarrassed about the first time we were together and I jizzed before I ever got the chance for her to touch me.

I can't let that happen again…not when I need to be inside her as bad as I do right now.

She's getting close, and I have the sudden need to feel her cunt pulsing around me as she lets go. I pull my hand out of her and flip her onto her back so swiftly she barely has time to register what's happening. I climb over her and snap her panties off her body as I pull my dick out, sliding it straight into her as she wraps her legs around my back, urging me into her with her feet digging into my ass.

I drive into her, and she falls apart after only a few pumps in. I feel that sweet, sweet pussy as it clenches over me, her moans turning into cries as she clutches the sheets between her fingertips and comes hard all over my cock.

I watch her gorgeous face as it screws up, twisting in pleasure at the feel of me, of what we're doing, of what I'm doing to her. God damn, I love making her come, and I love making her smile, and I just love her. Hard.

I'm hit with the realization that not only am I banging Alexis Bodega, but *she loves me,* and *I love her.* This wave of emotion plows through me as my balls tighten and the fire roars fiercely through me.

I start to come, a string of curses falling from my lips as I burst inside of her. I drive into her a little harder as her body greedily milks every last drop of my come, and as I start to come down from the high and my body feels completely depleted, I collapse over her. She wraps her arms around me tightly, holding on as if she never wants to let me go—as if she never wants me to let go, either.

And if she didn't have somewhere to be today, maybe I never *would* let go.

But I have to.

I slip out of her, and it's too dark to see my come as it slides down her slit, but I can imagine it, and I'm very nearly already hard again just at the thought of it.

I kiss her neck greedily, and then we both get up and head for the shower. I tenderly clean her body, and she does mine, and it's another first with her. I've showered with women before, but never as a tender and loving act. Everything with her is different, and *that* is why I don't care how long it takes until we can be together.

I'm not going anywhere.

Chapter 8
Danny

We don't get a whole lot of time together during the day on Tuesday. She's busy filming her scenes, and I'm supposed to fade into the background. I'm playing myself, a part I was literally born to play, and I'm walking by in the background with a gorgeous woman on my arm for today.

Tomorrow I'll have one line to speak to Alexis—or Charity, as she's called in the movie—where I hit on her and she declines because she's trapped in her own life, and then I choose the woman beside her and move on.

It's art imitating life in so many ways it's scary…except she didn't decline when I hit on her, and there are zero women I'd ever choose over her.

As far as everyone around her knows, though, she *did* decline when it came to me. As far as everyone knows, she's going to end up with Brooks. And in the film, it's an added layer to her character where she regrets the loss of yet another potential relationship.

She's not going to lose me, though.

I will fight to hell and back for her. For us. That's how real and important this has become to me in such a short amount of time.

The gorgeous woman on my arm is Kit Davenport—the same Kit Davenport of reality TV fame who's now apparently trying to break into Hollywood. I've not met her before, but she isn't shy about the fact that she wants to hang out between takes.

And I'm not quite sure how to handle that.

The Danny of a year ago wouldn't have thought twice about it. We'd have already found a nice, quiet place to fuck.

But the Danny of today has different priorities. The problem is the rest of the world hasn't caught up to that fact yet since those priorities changed in secret.

When it's a lunch break, I sneak into Alexis's trailer.

"Kit asked for my number," I announce, and she glances up at me from her spot on the couch and rolls her eyes. She sets the script she was reviewing on the end table beside her.

"Tell her it's taken."

I laugh. "I would, but then she'll ask by who, and then I'll have to tell her, and then the secret about you and Brooks will come out…"

"You don't have to tell her anything. Just tell her you're not interested." She purses her lips and eyes me a bit pointedly.

"Wait a second," I say, walking over and standing in front of her. "Are you…are you jealous?"

She folds her arms over her chest, and I'm not going to lie…she's currently in the perfect seat to unzip my pants, pull my cock out, and suck away.

"No, I'm not *jealous*," she says, her tone definitely exasperated.

"Maybe you should be." I toss her a wink to let her know I'm just kidding.

She leans back and glares up at me a little. "Fine. Then maybe I am. But I have exactly zero room to be considering the fact that I'm marrying some other guy in eighteen days."

I push the idea of a quick BJ out of my head as I collapse on the couch beside her. "This is all so fucked."

"Yeah," she murmurs, and she leans her head on my shoulder. "Maybe I'd be jealous if I didn't literally wake up to morning sex with you today."

"You have no reason to be jealous."

"The fact that you came in here and told me speaks volumes about that, Danny. You could've just as easily hid it," she points out.

"I'm glad you see it that way. I'd never want to hide anything from you, and I guess I'm trying to figure out how to let her down gently."

She reaches over and squeezes my hand. "Thank you."

I lean down and press a kiss to the top of her head. "You're welcome. For what, exactly?"

She chuckles. "For being you. For being honest with me. For sticking by me even though it's beyond confusing being with me."

"The confusion is worth it for the sweet moments of total clarity," I say softly.

A knock sounds at her door, and she glances at me. "Probably my next call."

"I'll slip out after you," I say.

She nods and presses a soft kiss to my lips before she gets up, picks up her script, and answers the door.

But it's not her next call at all.

"Brooks!" she says, surprise evident in her tone. "What are you doing here?"

Brooks? What the fuck is he doing here?

I watch as she seems to physically shrink down to a shell of who she is when she's with me. The expressiveness, the joy, the happiness…it all fades away as a weight seems to press her into someone else.

He answers the question in my head.

"Your father sent me to check on you. We both knew you were worried about him and with the wedding approaching, we both thought it would be good for us to be seen together. Can I come in?"

She still hasn't invited him in—likely because she doesn't want him to know I'm in here. He'll report back to her father, and it'll be nothing but trouble.

But she doesn't have a choice. She steps back to allow him in and looks at me wide-eyed.

"Danny?" Brooks says as he walks in and sees me sitting on her couch.

I clear my throat and stand, offering a nod. "Brooks."

"What's he doing here?" he asks Alexis. "Is he bothering you?"

She shakes her head. "No, no. He has a small role in this film, and he's shooting today and tomorrow. He stopped by for a visit. Wasn't that nice?" She's a little high-pitched in the lie, but mostly, she's putting on a pretty good act. But she's perfected the act now, right? If her goal is to win an Academy Award, why not put it on in all aspects of life?

Just…not with me.

"Yeah," Brooks says, narrowing his eyes at me. "Nice."

I don't mean to hit her when she's already down, but I put the act on, too. "Kit's probably wondering where I went. I better get back to set. Nice seeing you, Alexis." I nod at Brooks again.

"And you, Mr. Brewer," she says rather formally, the eyes that fall onto me so warmly riddled with confusion and fear.

On Deck

And then I walk out of her trailer, sure I'm doing the wrong thing by leaving her alone with him, but also sure I don't have any other choice.

Chapter 9
Alexis

"What was he really doing in here, Alexis?" Brooks demands as soon as the door closes behind Danny.

"He has a small role," I repeat. I force myself to school my reaction right now. I can't have him finding anything out I don't want him to know.

"Okay, fine. He has a small role. That does not explain why he's in your trailer between takes," he points out.

"He's a friend, Brooks. He's a nice guy who stopped by to say hi since we're in the same town filming the same movie." I go for exasperation on purpose when the truth is I'm beyond exasperated.

I already know he's going to tell my father. I really can't wait for that call, by the way.

"Why are you really here?" I ask him.

"Your dad was worried. He said you sounded stressed when you last spoke," he says.

Right. Because he's forcing this wedding on me in eighteen days. I *am* stressed. I'm panicked. I'm nervous. I'm scared. I'm all the things a bride *should* be eighteen days before her wedding…except I'm marrying the wrong man.

I wish there was some magic solution for all this, but I have yet to find it.

And the truth is that either my dad found out about Danny, and that's why he sent Brooks, or he suspects I'm up to something. He's finding some way to ensure I really go through with this. He's pressing his thumb over me just like he does when we're at home.

He's putting me back in the prison he keeps me in, and I have no way to escape.

I can't even if I wanted to. I already agreed to the stupid wedding.

"He also wanted me to get your opinion on a few details about the wedding," he says. "We agreed that while he has a good feel for your preferences and he's shared that with the wedding planner, you should have a hand in some of the final details."

I blow out a breath. "Why? You two are forcing me into this. I don't care what you pick. Just pick."

His brows quirk. "I'm sorry you feel that way, Alexis."

It almost feels like my feelings on the subject are a surprise to him.

"Do *you* want this?" I ask.

"I'm on board with the merger, and of course I care deeply about you."

"As a *wife*, though?" I press.

He blows out a breath as he averts his eyes to the ground for a beat, and I get the very real sense that he's never *actually* let me in. He's keeping something from me, and I don't like it.

"Brooks?" I ask.

He finally glances up at me. "Love, relationships...I guess I've always viewed them as business decisions. And I thought you were the same. I thought we were cut from the same cloth."

Maybe I was. But then I met Danny.

I'm not anymore.

I can't tell Brooks that, though.

I press my lips together and nod. "It's for the brand," I say softly.

He nods. "It'll put you front and center in the news. It'll raise your stock. It'll garner new fans because of the designer you choose for your dress or the music you choose for our first dance."

"I didn't choose *any* of it," I roar. I'm not sure where the deep emotion comes from, but I hope I can channel back to it at another point because there's a scene in the movie coming up when we're back in Los Angeles that rings very similar to this conversation right now.

"I know," he says. "And all that's already been chosen anyway. Your dad just wanted to know who you wanted to be your maid of honor."

"He doesn't have any business contacts for that?" I spit.

"There needs to be *some* personal touches to make it believable."

Only one name springs to mind.

Danny's sister, Anna.

It's not like I can share that name with Brooks. It's not like I can ask her, either—not when she knows the truth. She can't stand up in support of me marrying another man when she knows how her brother feels about me...and how I feel about him.

I'm not really all that close to any other women, except I sort of led my father to believe I am. "I don't have anyone in mind."

"What about Leila Monroe?" he asks, naming my co-star.

It'll help promote this movie if we show a united front as I marry Brooks during filming.

One more lie. One more façade. One more manipulation.

I hate all of it.

But the wheels are already in motion, and I have no idea how to stop any of it. "I don't care."

Brooks picks up his phone. "Mr. Bodega, hello. Alexis has chosen Leila Monroe as her maid of honor." I can't hear my father's side of the conversation, but Brooks says, "Yes, she's right here. Of course." He hands me the phone.

"Dad?" I say as I hold it up to my ear.

"Alexis, that's a fine choice, and a smart one, too."

"Thanks," I mutter.

"Are you okay? You seemed upset last night when you hung up on me."

The accusation is there, and it's not untrue. I did hang up on him when I started having a panic attack thinking about this stupid sham of a wedding, and those same feelings are starting to unfurl in my periphery now that Brooks is here and Danny is…with Kit?

He wouldn't. I know he wouldn't. I know he mentioned her to throw Brooks off our scent.

I shouldn't feel sick at the thought. He deserves someone who he doesn't have to wait for.

Still, I hate thinking that he ran to her.

"I'm okay. I need to get back to set soon, so I'll pass you back to Brooks, okay?"

"Okay, sweetheart. Love you."

I mumble it back and hand the phone back to Brooks.

"Sir, one more thing," he says as I absently flip through the script. "When I arrived at your daughter's trailer, she was in here alone with Danny Brewer."

Dammit.

On Deck

Really, Brooks?
What a fucking traitor.

Chapter 10
Danny

This feels bad.

Really bad.

I'm trying to respect that she wants to hide what we have from not just the world but specifically her father, and there is no way in hell Brooks isn't going to run straight to him to let him know he caught us.

He doesn't know what he caught, though, and I'm banking on that.

I don't dare text her even though I want to let her know it's okay. Instead, I wait it out.

And I will also do my part to ensure the world never makes the connection between us.

There's a lounge where those of us with small parts in this movie get to chill between takes, and I head that direction since I know it's where Kit will be.

We share all our scenes, so if I'm not on set right now, she isn't, either. She's chatting with Natasha Prince—the same reality TV star who filmed the Hush commercial with Alexis and me.

She stands when I walk in, and she gives me a hug.

"Good to see you," she says, and I echo the same sentiment.

"You two know each other?" Kit asks.

"We met a few weeks ago on a commercial shoot," Natasha says. The Hush NDA we signed was pretty strict, so better to keep it vague. She gives me a look that I'm a little confused about, but I take it to mean I shouldn't ask how things are going with The Gamer.

"You two know each other?" I ask, nodding between the two of them.

"We were both associated with Netflix," Kit says. "We were just catching up." She smiles at me as if she's ready to be done catching up with Natasha since I'm back.

"I was just going to grab some lunch if you'd like to join me," I say against my better judgment. I glance at Natasha by way of extending the invitation to her as well. I can't help but wonder how much she thinks she knows about me from our time in the Hush house. I may have come off as rather standoffish to everyone except Alexis while we were there since my entire focus was on not spilling the beans about the woman I was falling for.

"I'd love to," Kit says, and Natasha nods.

The three of us make our way toward the buffet tables set up for the cast and crew. They each make themselves a salad, and I grab a ham and cheese sandwich from the pile of subs.

We find a table and sit together, chatting about nothing, but at least I'm being seen with someone other than Alexis.

Alexis is right, though—the insider details about what happens on set won't make their way public. It's when we're outside filming and the public can see us that pictures are snapped, which is why it was so smart of Gregory to drive her to my place rather than letting me do it.

But the secrets are getting harder to maintain, especially when her *fiancé* shows up unannounced.

The lines are getting blurry as the promises I made to myself about getting involved with a woman involved with someone else are broken. I keep telling myself she's not *really* involved with him. She doesn't love him.

But does it matter?

I'm not the guy who cares what other people think of me. I never have been.

But this is something else entirely. This is showing the entire world I think deception and cheating are okay, and that reflects back on me as a ballplayer, too. If I can do it in my personal life, it's not much of a stretch to think I'd do it on the field.

And I would never do that. I play honorably. Always. And I try to live my life that way, too—without getting tangled up in the webs others seem to find themselves in.

Along came Alexis, blowing up everything I thought I always believed in. I can't stay away. I *won't* stay away. I hate the hiding. I hate how this is going to reflect on me. But I love her more than I care about any of that.

"What about you, Danny?" Kit asks. She sets her palm on my bicep, and I want to shake it off. It's not her bicep to touch.

I suck in a breath as I realize I have no idea what she just asked me. I guess I was lost in my own thoughts. "I'm sorry. What?"

"How's your lunch?" she repeats. She gives me a strange look.

I hold up my sandwich that I've nearly wolfed down at this point. "Fine. Yours?"

Kit and Natasha exchange a look. Fine, so they must've just been talking about how good or bad or mediocre their salad is, and I wasn't paying a single bit of attention. They'll think I'm a dumb jock who can't hold a conversation.

Now *that* is something I couldn't care less about.

"When's your next call?" Natasha asks, and I force myself to be present in the conversation.

"Kit and I have another forty-five minutes," I say.

"I have fifteen minutes until my next one," she says.

We shoot the shit for a few more minutes, and then she heads back to set. I grab an energy drink, and Kit and I hang out.

"You want to go out somewhere tonight?" she asks.

I shrug. Since Brooks is in town, it appears my other plans have folded. "Sure. But I should tell you…I'm not the guy I used to be, Kit. I think you are gorgeous, and a year ago, I wouldn't have hesitated. But tonight, this is just us going out as friends. It can't be more than that."

She twists her lips with a bit of disappointment. "Okay. But can we take photos pretending like it's more than that? Because I have an ex who is a huge fan of the Heat, and I would *love* to rub our new friendship in his face."

I laugh, and honestly…it's not a bad idea. We give the press something to focus on, throw shade off any potential rumors about Alexis and me, and put on an act specifically for Brooks and Alexis's father…and Kit's ex. "Yeah. I think we can definitely do that."

I'm not quite sure what I just agreed to, but I guess I'll find out later tonight. I'm thankful she doesn't ask me *why* I'm not interested, but I'm not sure I'll get off so easily tonight.

And I don't.

I don't see Alexis for the rest of the day. She's obviously being kept under tight watch now that Brooks is here, and I hate it. I still don't dare to text her knowing he's so close, and I'm not sure what else to do.

On Deck

I hang around as long as humanly acceptable, but ultimately, I have to leave. I have no other excuses left. And so when we're done filming for the day, Kit and I grab an Uber over to Skip's, the bar near the stadium where I always hang with Coop, Rush, and AJ, and it sort of feels like being home again.

I slide into my usual corner booth, and Kelly comes by and snags my usual order.

"You haven't been around much lately, Danny," she says.

"Been busy," I say, which is definitely a total non-excuse.

"Rush and Coop haven't, either, but AJ is in here almost every night."

"Glad to see he's keeping you open," I say, offering a friendly smile as she scampers away to get our drinks.

The night feels pretty usual, but what's *not* so usual about tonight is the fact that I'm here with a pseudo-celebrity, one that has a huge and rather rabid fanbase.

"How'd you like filming today?" I ask, trying to make conversation.

"I had a blast with you," she says, leaning in a little closer—probably to give off whatever vibe she wants the rest of the world to perceive.

To be honest, I'm really, really tired of these games. When I took the route of baseball as the road I wanted to travel for the rest of my life, I didn't really consider the *celebrity* side of it.

"I think the director liked me, and I'm hoping it leads to more opportunities," she says. "What about you? How'd you get involved with this film?"

I lift a shoulder. "Long story." It's not, but I'm not going to get into it with *Kit*, a person I just met, at a bar where anybody could overhear us.

Kelly drops our drinks, and she has barely cleared the end of our table before another fan approaches Kit. She's asked for an autograph. And then she's asked for a selfie. And then more approach us. Most people don't even really pay all that much attention to the dude sitting in the booth with her…at first.

But then I'm recognized, and it feels like all hell breaks loose.

Photo after photo is snapped, and Kit plays into it the entire time, leaning into me, flirting, and just generally putting on an act like we're here together. People can read into it whatever they want, and that was the whole goal for her tonight, wasn't it?

I don't want anyone reading anything into any of it, but what other choice do I have? I'm doing this for Alexis—for us, to make sure her dad and Brooks aren't sniffing around us.

The only problem is that in order to continue protecting her, I have no way of letting her know that whatever rumors make their way into the universe after this…none of it is true.

And the longer I sit here with Kit, the more concerned that makes me.

Chapter 11
Alexis

I pace back and forth across the room at the hotel where the studio is putting us up.

It's a nice enough room—a suite, actually, on the top floor overlooking Las Vegas Boulevard—but admittedly, I have not yet seen the inside of it since I've been with Danny.

Gregory saved my ass by making sure my suitcase was at the hotel and I had my room key, and I have never been more grateful for him. He's covering for me, and I never expected him to. I never asked him to.

It means a lot to know he's on my side. He's the only one in my circle who is.

Maybe he even *likes* Danny. Or maybe he *doesn't* like Brooks. But if it's his job to protect me, I don't think it's too much of a stretch to think he'd be invested in protecting my heart, too.

And clearly he sees that what I have with Danny is not the same thing I have with Brooks. It gives me a whole lot of faith that Gregory knows me as well as he does and believes I'm making the right choice.

"Are you going to pace all night?" Brooks asks, irritation evident in his tone.

"I'm nervous about tomorrow's shoot," I lie.

"Why?"

"I'd rather not talk about it." *I'd rather not lie more about it.*

I blow out a breath and pick up my script to read over my lines again.

I know them. That's not the issue.

I'm nervous about what Danny is up to tonight. I'm nervous about what tomorrow will look like. I just want Brooks to leave, but he's hanging around like a bad cold and hasn't said how long he plans to stay in Vegas. Doesn't he have work to do back in Los Angeles? Shouldn't he be getting ready for the merger? Why is he here?

Oh, right.

To babysit me.

And apparently to wedding plan, too.

"I talked to your dad before. Rafe has three dress choices for you when you have a moment to choose," he says.

"Rafe?" I repeat. I have no idea who that is.

"The wedding planner."

"Oh, right. Sure, I can take a look now, I guess."

"You guess?" he says. "I thought you were on board with this, Alexis."

I heave out a breath. I don't want to be rude to Brooks, but I feel like my future husband should have some semblance of how I'm feeling right now.

I'm about to tell him how I am on board, and it's fine, and…whatever it is, I need to say to give him the reassurance he's seeking, but he plows ahead first.

On Deck

"Does this have anything to do with Brewer?" He narrows his eyes at me.

"What if it does?" I ask.

"You said he was a friend. How'd he snag a role in this film?"

I shrug as I realize I've become a better liar than I thought. "Coincidence."

He studies me for a beat as if he doesn't really believe me, and he's trying to get to the bottom of the truth. I tip my chin up and stand confidently in front of him.

"Right." He presses his lips together. "You need to stay away from him. If word got out that you two are *friends*, it would be really bad for the brand."

I don't give two flying shits about the brand.

He's good for my *heart*.

And that's what it comes down to.

Brooks and my dad are pitting me against *myself*—me against my own brand. But my brand is what *they* have built for me. It was *their* vision.

And frankly…I'm tired of living out someone else's vision.

I'm ready to take control.

I just have to take Brooks's last name first so I can ensure I have the rights that belong to me.

I need an air-tight prenup that I have someone outside of my father's lawyers review for me before I sign it.

And then, when the dust settles, when the merger is finalized so the divorce can be finalized…then Danny and I can finally be together.

"Did you see these?" Brooks asks, interrupting my thoughts. He flashes his phone at me, and my chest tightens at the first picture.

Danny is smiling as he sits in a booth at some bar next to Kit Davenport. Her hand is on his arm, and he's looking at her the way he should be looking at me. The headline mentions the bad boy of baseball once again.

He's not a bad boy.

He's one of the good ones…one of the *few* good ones I've ever come across in my life.

I believe in us. I trust him.

This isn't one of those silly miscommunications where I see him out with another woman and assume he's up to no good.

I know Danny. I know his heart. I know the love he has for me. And I will trust in that until the day I die.

I won't let these photographs get to me.

He's out there doing what he has to do to keep Brooks happy, and Brooks is only shoving this in my face to make his point.

I won't let him see me sweat.

"Looks like a fun time." I shoot him a sugary smile, and for as much as this guy thinks he knows me…he has no idea how fake that smile really is.

And I'm further confident in what I feel in my heart when a text from Gregory comes through.

It's in a code that only I would understand, but it's further evidence that placing my trust in Danny is the right thing to do.

Gregory: *Leo's uncle assured me he only wants bacon.*

Leo's uncle is Danny…and we love to share bacon.

I have nothing to worry about. The fact that he texted Gregory instead of me only proves he's forcing himself to stay away while Brooks is here.

"Show me the dresses," I say with renewed enthusiasm.

Because the sooner I say *I do*, and the sooner this merger is complete…the sooner I can get divorced. And then I can finally be with Danny in every way that matters.

Chapter 12
Danny

Gregory said she responded to his text last night with a thumbs up, which I took to mean that she got the message and she knows why I did what I had to do.

I get to the set early the next morning, but I don't see her right away. In fact, she's stuck in her trailer with Brooks tailing her, and the only time I *do* get to see her on set, Brooks is watching her every move.

I force myself not to look at her. I force myself to sling an arm around Kit, and to really put my all into the act. This is my last day of shooting—they only needed me for two—but Alexis will be here through Friday.

I wish I could be with her. I wish I had more days to shoot. I wish we could share a scene aside from the one we filmed yesterday.

Instead, I'm a backdrop, and I only had the one line to share with her.

But as her character's eyes edge over toward me with my arm around Kit as she snuggles into my chest, I can't help but feel like the disdain in her eyes is not much of an act at all and instead is very, very real.

I do my best to keep my eyes off her between takes so Brooks doesn't think anything is up, and I keep my eyes on Kit instead.

Kit is preening, and Alexis is pushing it all into her acting, and somehow it's working.

I head home for the day when my scenes are over, one part glad I won't have to return tomorrow and the other part upset I won't have time with Alexis tomorrow.

Kit offered another night out with me. I declined. I just want to go home and hope that Brooks leaves sooner than later.

I haven't heard from her all day, so I assume Brooks is still here. It's a little after ten when I hear a knock at my front door, and I'm three beers into my solo night despite a couple different offers to go out.

Honestly, though, those offers are coming fewer and further between. I guess when you decline enough times, people stop asking. I didn't really feel any sort of decrease in offers until I was sitting here alone with no way to get in touch with my girlfriend except through her bodyguard. Even when the offers did come in—one from Rush for a poker night with him and Coop, and one from AJ to hit up a club—I didn't think twice when I declined either one.

I open the door and find Alexis Bodega standing on my front porch in a hoodie with the hood pulled up over her hair.

She rushes straight into my arms, and I wave to Gregory in the driveway before he nods.

I close the door behind her, holding onto her with one arm as she clings to me.

I gaze down at her, and when her eyes meet mine, I see relief in them. She presses her lips to mine for just a beat.

"I hated that, Danny," she says, and she kisses me again. "I hated seeing you with Kit." Another kiss. "I hated those pictures all over the internet." Kiss. "But I believe you," kiss, "and I trust you," kiss, "and I trust *us*," kiss, "and I knew you were just doing what you had to do."

I push her hood down then thread my fingertips into her hair and hold the back of her head to kiss her good and hard, the way a woman deserves to be kissed. I open my mouth, and her tongue immediately moves to brush against mine, dancing and exploring each other sweetly at first, but the urgency moves in quickly.

My body feels that sense of urgency, too, and I reach under her to pull her up so her legs are linked around my waist. I buck my hips toward her, and we both grunt at the feel as my rock-hard cock begs for entrance with far too many clothes separating us.

I need her. I need this. I crave the intimacy I've only ever shared with her.

My balls ache with need, and I carry her into the kitchen and perch her on the edge of the counter. It's a little high, but I'm tall enough to make it work. I flick the button of her jeans then lower them with her panties down her legs. I toss them onto the floor, and I lean down and pepper kisses along the inside of her thigh. She braces herself by leaning back with her palms flat on the counter behind her, which only sticks her chest out toward me.

And it would be a damn shame to let those sweet tits go without a little attention. I straighten and yank off her hoodie and shirt then unclasp her bra, and she's naked on my kitchen counter, and I am one goddamn lucky man.

My brain is in a fog as I try to figure out which way to go with her first. I want to take my time. I want to take all fucking night. But the pulse in my balls is telling another story entirely.

And so I suck one of her tits into my mouth, and she arches into me as I shove a finger into her sweet, tight pussy. I want to taste her again, but the urge to fuck her right here on my counter is too strong.

She's moaning as she grinds her hips against my hand, and I can't take it any longer. I need her hips grinding against my cock.

I pull my hands out, and her reaction is a strangled moan of desperation, but I quickly work my cock out of the basketball shorts I'm wearing and stroke it a couple of times before I push her thighs apart and slide into her hot, tight cunt.

She's so wet that I slide in and out with ease over and over, and she's still leaning back on her palms with her tits arched toward me so I can bend down and angle my head to get one in my mouth. With her pussy filled with my dick and my mouth filled with her tit, I'm pretty damn sure this is heaven.

It's pure perfection. It's all of her consuming all of me, and it's exactly what I've needed the last two days as I fought against the fears that Brooks was coming between us.

She would never let that happen. I know her well enough to know that, and the fact that we both believed in each other despite time apart tells me exactly what I needed to know.

I've never felt this level of trust with another human being, and it's perfect and beautiful. But most of all, it's forever.

I push into her over and over, harder and harder, and it feels so good, so consuming, so fiery hot all at once. I listen to her moans as our bodies slap together, and she starts to get a little louder—always the sign that she's getting close.

I move my lips from her tits and press my mouth to hers, and she reaches up around my neck to cling onto me as I drive into her even harder.

Her cunt tightens all around me, a vice as she squeezes me so hard I slip right into my climax.

On Deck

I start to come, and I grunt her name softly paired with a string of curses as I spill into her. "Oh, fuck, Lex, yes. I'm coming all over your hot cunt. You're mine, Lex. Fucking mine."

"Yes!" she screams as she comes right along with me. "Yes, yours, Danny. All yours. Only yours."

Her words are a vow, just as mine are to her.

I may have to share her with Brooks for now, but in the end…it'll be her and me. We will find a way.

Chapter 13
Alexis

I cling onto him as we both pant in the afterglow, and eventually he slips out of me but doesn't let me go. His hot come slides out of me, making an absolute wreckage of the kitchen counter, but rather than worry about cleaning it up tonight, we'll deal with it tomorrow.

He carries me upstairs and through the bedroom to the shower, where we stand together under the hot spray of water as his mouth finds mine. He kisses me slowly, his arms linked around me as he holds me close, and I'm not sure I've ever felt more content than I do in this moment.

It's this intimacy we share that I've never had before, and it's the very thing I hold onto in the moments when we can't be together. I've never been kissed like this before—like the man kissing me is worshipping me, and it's not about publicity or money or fame, but it's about the intense connection we share. This kiss is our expression of the love and adoration we both feel, this beautiful and perfect love neither of us has ever shared with anyone before.

And it's that exact feeling that helps me through the dark times—it's that exact feeling that drives this understanding in me that somehow, we will figure this out.

We will fight whatever battles we need to in order to end up together because this is where we belong.

He dries me tenderly and hands me one of his Vegas Heat t-shirts to sleep in. It's soft and smells like him, and I climb into his bed feeling utterly happy.

I smile at him as he climbs in beside me, and we face each other, heads on pillows as his eyes meet mine.

"Are you tired?" he asks.

"Exhausted," I admit. "Brooks had about a million questions today about the wedding, none of which I wanted to answer."

"Then why did you?"

"Because I have to." I lift the shoulder I'm not laying on as some of the happiness and contentedness seem to dampen. "I have to get this over with. The sooner it's all done, the sooner you and I can finally be together."

He narrows his eyes for a beat and opens his mouth to say something, but the words don't come out. Instead, he seems to think twice about it and then asks, "What kinds of questions did you have to answer?"

"Which dress I liked best of the three options my father gave me. Playlists for the reception. Most of the choices were made for me already, but my dad wanted me to feel like I had some hand in the plans. I don't want a hand in the plans. I don't want to do it at all." I keep my eyes steady on his so he knows I'm speaking from the heart.

It's hard saying the words. I'm sure it's even harder to hear them.

His brows push together, and I get the sense he's not saying something again.

"What?" I ask.

"If you don't want to marry him, then...don't," he says.

I sigh. "It's not quite that simple. If I do this, I get my masters back. I get a new agent. I make my dad happy, and he's worked hard his whole life to make *me* happy. I just have to do this one thing." My voice is subdued as I say the words I keep thinking. Danny is the *only* person I'd ever actually voice any of that to.

"It *is* that simple, Lex," he says softly. "You only get one life. You should get to make your own decisions."

I press my lips together. "I am. And this is what I'm deciding."

"But there has to be another way, don't you think?" he presses.

"I guess I just...feel like I'm out of options at this point. Maybe there is, but my dad landing in the hospital put it in perspective for me. I have to do this. What if I lost him? What if he never got to see his dreams through because he died in that hospital room?" I feel the pulse of heat behind my eyes.

"He didn't, though. He's still here fighting another day. And it's not fair for you to give up on your dreams at the expense of his."

He's right. Deep down, I know that.

But that doesn't mean I can change any of it.

"If you're willing to stick by me through this, however long it takes, then I'm not giving up on my dreams," I say. "I'm just delaying them a little so in the end, we can all benefit."

"Except for me," he says softly.

I tilt my head forward to press my lips to his. "I'm sorry, Danny."

He closes his eyes and draws in a deep breath, and I hate that I feel this wedge between us. I thought he was okay with all of this, but clearly…he isn't.

And I'm not sure how to fix that since opting out of the wedding at this point feels completely out of the question.

"I love you," he says softly.

"I love you, too." I press my lips to his again, and then we both attempt to fall asleep.

I don't sleep at all, though.

Instead, I toss and turn as I search for some solution that will fix all of this.

When daylight dawns, I'm no closer to any answers.

And when my alarm rings at five, I see I have a text from Gregory.

Gregory: *Your call time was changed to noon. I'll pick you up at ten-thirty unless I hear from you.*

I turn off my alarm and try to get some sleep, but it's useless. I head down to the kitchen, where I spray some bleach onto the counter and clean up from last night.

I find some bacon in the fridge, lay it on a baking sheet, and put it in the oven.

Danny saunters down a little before six looking both very sexy and very sleepy. "I felt like I was in one of those old cartoons where the bacon scent wafts up the stairs and the character follows his nose down to the kitchen."

I giggle. "It'll be ready any minute."

"Do you have any idea how sexy you look wearing just my shirt?" he asks.

I glance down doubtfully at the huge shirt that looks like a potato sack on me. "Really?"

He chuckles as he walks over to me and slings his arm around my neck, pulling me in close. "You really are the best, do you know that?"

I lift a modest shoulder.

He presses a kiss on my cheek. "I think you might just be my favorite person in the whole world."

For some reason, his words cause tears to spring to my eyes. Maybe it's because I realize for the first time that I feel the exact same way.

He's not just my favorite person.

He's my person.

We feast on bacon paired with scrambled eggs, and I get dressed even though I sort of want to stay in his shirt forever.

It's inching closer to ten-thirty, and Danny holds me in his arms about ten minutes before Gregory is scheduled to arrive for pickup.

He presses a soft kiss on my forehead. "I'll stay away today, but let it be known I don't want to."

"I don't want you to, either." I tighten my arms around his waist. "But I'll have Gregory bring me back here as soon as filming wraps for the day."

"I'm holding you to that. I'll be waiting." He shoves his hips against mine. "And I'll be horny."

I laugh. "Same."

A knock sounds at the door, and I look up at Danny and make a sad face, and he kisses my pouty lip. Then he turns me around and swats my ass, sending me toward the door where Gregory waits.

I throw it open with a laugh, only...

It's not Gregory standing there.

My brows dip as the man standing there most definitely recognizes me, shock on his face as his jaw drops. My eyes reach his as his jaw closes and his lips curl into a menacing smile, and the first thing I notice is that his eyes are the exact same blue as...

"Dad?" Danny breathes, disbelief in his tone. "What the fuck are you doing here?"

Chapter 14
Danny

My chest feels like someone set a crushing weight on top of it.

I haven't spoken to him in four years. I haven't *seen* him in four years, and he looks…different. Older. Thinner, as if he's lost some weight. But also a bit like he's aged an entire decade in the last four years.

The last time I saw him was in Los Angeles. I was in the off-season after my third year in the MLB, and he showed up at the same bar I was at. I still don't know how he tracked me there, but he cornered me, gave me some sob story, and asked me for money.

I told him no. I told him I didn't want anything to do with him ever again.

I was hoping that would be the end of it. Clearly I was wrong.

Why the hell would he show up right now?

What the hell does he want from me?

Oh, right...money. That's all he ever wanted. The woman he cheated on my mother with had more money than my angel of a mother did, and so he chose the other woman. It wasn't for *love*.

He had no idea I'd become a professional baseball player with a bigger paycheck than he could ever dream of. But considering all he ever was to me was the sperm donor my mom unfortunately married, I don't feel like I owe him a goddamn thing.

Until his next words tell me I'm definitely going to owe him *something* in order to hold onto his silence.

Fuck. Fuck!

"Wow, Alexis Bodega," he says. "I had no idea you were a friend of my son's."

All the color drains from her face, and a Yukon pulls into the driveaway a moment later.

Thank God Gregory is here to get her out of here, but I have no idea how I'm going to keep my father quiet.

"She's in town filming a movie I scored a small role in," I say, scrambling for an explanation. "She came by for breakfast before she heads home to her fiancé."

"Right," he says, drawing out the word with a heavy dose of sarcasm as if he doesn't believe a word I'm saying.

"I need to get back to the shoot. Nice to see you again, Danny," she says to me, offering me a tight smile before she pulls her hood up and runs out to the Yukon.

Gregory peels out of the driveway, and my father watches until he pulls around the corner.

"Aren't you going to invite your old man in?" he asks.

I press my lips together as I shake my head. "Wasn't planning on it."

"Well now that I have a little information at my disposal, I'm assuming you'll change your mind." It's a threat, and I wouldn't put it past him to act on it. He doesn't make empty threats.

He slips inside before I can close the door, and I sigh. Dealing with this asshole really wasn't on my agenda for the day.

"What are you doing here?" I repeat.

"I came to visit my son," he says, his tone definitely indicating that I'm a dummy for even asking that.

"You've never once in your life come to visit me just for the hell of it. Now get on with it. What the fuck do you want from me?"

"Olivia is graduating from college this spring, and Rebecca and I don't have enough to give her the sort of graduation present we always dreamed of giving her. So I came to you to ask for help," he admits.

"I'm not sure how that has anything to do with me," I say. I haven't moved from the front hall, but he's starting to wander around the entry. He makes his way through toward my kitchen.

He looks all around as he walks. "Nice place you got here."

"How'd you even figure out where I live?" I demand. I'm pretty good at keeping a tight lid on that sort of thing.

"Don't you worry about that." He pauses in front of my kitchen counter—the very same one where I fucked Alexis last night—and he leans forward on it, and I can't help but wish Alexis hadn't admitted she cleaned up this morning. I also wish he would get the fuck out of my house. "So are you going to help your half-sister or not?"

"Don't you dare call her that to me," I hiss. "You know what you did, and I will *never* forgive you for betraying Mom. For betraying *all* of us. You're dead to me. I don't have a father."

"Oh, come on, Danny-boy. It's been decades at this point. You're still hung up on all that shit?" His tone is flippant, and I could fucking slug the guy for his attitude.

"Have you ever walked in on someone having sex?" I ask, trying to paint a picture for him.

He shrugs. "Sure. Hasn't everybody?"

"Okay, well did you ever walk in on your dad, the man you were supposed to be able to trust above any other man in the world when he was sticking his dick in another woman when you were seven years old, and you didn't even know what sex was?" I demand. "Do you know how much that fucked me up? *That* is why I want nothing to do with you. You chose them, and when you chose them, you chose to write me out of your life. So stop fucking coming around here begging for handouts."

He folds his arms across his chest, and the confidence of this guy is appalling. "Let's not call it a *handout*, then, shall we?"

I fold my arms across my chest, too. I'm bigger than him, and I'm a professional athlete. I could take this guy with my eyes closed, and the longer he stands in my kitchen, the more I want to. "What would you prefer to call it?"

"A payment. For my silence."

"Your silence? For what?"

He twists his lips as he pretends to think about it. "Oh, you know. If you don't want anyone to know Alexis Bodega spent the night at your house last night."

"You don't know that." I roll my eyes.

He lifts a shoulder. "Does it matter? It's my word against yours, and you have a hell of a lot more to lose than I do."

I stare off at him for a beat as I try to figure out how to handle this.

There's just one problem.

When he got here this morning, he had no idea he'd run into Alexis. He didn't know he'd have something to hold over me.

So why did he show up here in the first place? What's really going on here? He wants money for Olivia's graduation gift, so he says.

But I know him and know there must be more to it.

"Why are you here?" I ask, shifting the topic.

"I told you. Olivia's graduation gift." Right. So he's sticking to that story.

"Exactly what are you buying her?" I ask. I walk around him to my fridge and grab an energy drink.

"A car."

"What kind of car?"

He lifts a shoulder. "Not sure, but I think it just got a little nicer given what I walked in on this morning."

I roll my eyes. "You can't really think blackmail is the answer here."

"It's not blackmail," he protests. "I told you, it's payment in exchange for something you want. Can I use your bathroom?"

"Fuck off out of here," I say. My phone starts to ring, and since I'd rather talk to just about anyone on Earth than this piece of scum, I pick it up. "Hey, Brad," I answer.

"Am I interrupting anything?" he asks.

"Nope. Fire away." I head outside to take this call, and he fills me in on how impressed the director was with my scenes yesterday, a new sponsorship opportunity, and three podcast spots coming up in the next few weeks.

By the time we're done, I'm hopeful my father has left.

He's not in the kitchen when I head back inside. I walk around the first floor and don't see him anywhere, and a minute later, he comes walking down the stairs.

"What the fuck do you think you're doing?" I ask.

"Checking out the place. Nice digs. I left my number on your counter. I'll be around," he says, letting himself out the front door.

I stare after the door for a beat, not really sure what happens next but glad he's gone.

I have a feeling he'll be back around soon enough, though.

LISA SUZANNE

And that scares the hell out of me.

Chapter 15
Alexis

I text Danny to let him know I'm coming...and also to make sure the coast is clear. I'm not entirely sure it's a good idea for me to head to his house when his dad was there earlier, but I also feel the pulsing need to *be there* for Danny.

I know it's been a while since he's seen his father. I want to make sure he's okay after all that.

He texts back to assure me that his dad is long gone.

He's waiting by the door when Gregory ushers me up the driveway.

It's late, and we're both tired. He ushers me straight up to his bedroom, and we both collapse into his bed without turning out the lights as we feel the need to just talk for a minute.

"Are you okay?" I ask him after he kisses me softly.

"Yes. No."

I nod as I lean on my elbow to hover over his face. "Same."

He huffs out a breath. "It's just...I put the deadbeat out of my head, you know? I don't let myself think about him or what he did to our entire family. He's as good as dead to me, but then he shows up out of fucking nowhere to stir shit up. We're already in this deep enough. We don't need his ass fucking things up even more."

I brush my fingertips along his forehead and back into his hairline softly then repeat the motion to try to soothe him. "You're right. We're barely hanging on here, and he's not going to make it any easier. But as long as we both feel what we feel…then we figure it out. We don't have any other choice."

"No, we don't. Because I'm not giving you up, Lex." His words push a warmth through my chest. "No matter what."

"Thank God for that. I'm not giving you up, either," I say.

"Can I ask you a question?"

I nod.

"You're working so hard to make your dad happy. But is this what your mom would have wanted for you?" he asks.

It's something I've thought a lot about, and ultimately…I know the answer. It's a tough pill to swallow, though. I shake my head. "No. She would've wanted me to be happy."

"Are you?" he asks.

"Only when I'm with you," I admit.

"Then leave him." He says the words so simply, but they're anything but simple.

It's too complicated. My father and I may have our differences, but ultimately what it comes down to is the fact that he's still my dad. Our relationship isn't like Danny's with his dad, and no amount of explaining will make him understand that.

My dad is the only person I've been able to trust my entire life, from when I was a kid to the success story I've become today.

The businesswoman in me says it's not smart to give that up for someone I've known for six months…no matter how right it feels.

No matter how much I want to.

No matter how much I *need* to.

He continues talking before I get the chance to say all that. "Leave Brooks publicly. Be with me…publicly. Stop the charade. Stop the fake relationship. Stop living your life as a way to please your father. He's always going to have excuses, Lex. The merger, joining two families, your agent, your masters. Next he'll claim you agreed to have kids with the guy. And I get why you feel like you have to do it, but let's just be happy. Be with me."

"I wish it was that easy," I admit. "I love you, Danny. You know how I feel about Brooks. I want to be with you more than anything. But I can't. I have to do this for my dad. He's the only family I have left."

He looks so disappointed that my heart very nearly can't take it.

I lean down and press my lips to his, and he grabs onto the back of my head, pulling me close as he kisses me like his life depends on it…like he'll be able to change my mind through his physicality.

If only it were that simple.

This kiss is intense, though, as if he snapped and needs to show me a different side of himself.

He shifts us so I'm face down on the bed, and he yanks my jeans down my legs and tosses them on the floor. He holds my head down by linking his fingers around my neck.

"You want something different tonight?" he asks. "Something rough?"

"Yes," I moan.

He shoves into me without any sort of foreplay, and it feels somehow both intimate and dirty at the same time—like he's trying to screw some sense into me to make me see things from his perspective while he dominates the hell out of my body.

But that's the thing…I *do* see what he's saying, and I absolutely agree with him. I'm just stuck in a place that I can't see my way out of.

He drives into me, and I'm flat on the bed, unable to move at all. His hand around the back of my neck holds me still, and the pure indecency of it all is somehow…hot?

Every drive in makes me somehow hotter. Wetter. Needier.

I cry out with the pain of it all, with the need to come, somehow matched beat for beat with the pleasure. It's overwhelming. For the first time ever, I think I understand that old phrase *hurts so good*. Because it's *so* damn good as he pushes into me, that throbbing ache building to a crescendo that's more and more agonizing with every thrust he makes.

He pulls out of me for a beat, the ache heavy and nearly unbearable, and he slides his dick up a little until he's probing at my ass. He doesn't push in, but just feeling the tiniest bit of pressure there undoes me.

The second he slides back down inside me, I start to come, my body betraying me as I crash headfirst into a crushing, brutal climax. I don't want to come. I want to revel in this beautiful torture forever, but just like everything always does, it comes to an end. I claw at the sheets, unable to move since he's holding me down, and it's the most violently powerful orgasm I've ever experienced in my twenty-eight years on this earth.

His thrusts start to pulse faster and deeper as he gets closer to his own release, and when it comes, he lets out a loud growl before he pulls out of me and jerks himself off all over my ass.

He grunts through his climax, the heat of his come splattering on my body, and when the jets stop pulsing out of him, he rubs the head of his dick through the semen he left behind.

It's the single hottest, most erotic moment of my life as I try to come down from the blissful cloud where I find myself.

On Deck

He just completely dominated me and my body. He obliterated me.

And the only thought in my mind is how much I want him to do that again.

Chapter 16
Danny

I'm not sure what that was.

It was this primal need I've never felt before to stake my claim and mark my territory in a way that honestly scared me a little.

I wanted to slide into her ass and claim that as mine, too. I was in such a lust-driven haze that I nearly did...but I know she's not ready for that yet.

Except, I think she wants it.

She *liked* it. There's no doubt about that. She liked how I completely dominated her. She liked how I held her down. She liked that I teased her ass.

She screamed when she came, and I don't even know if she realized she did it.

It was the fiercest, most primal and animalistic act I've ever shared with a woman, and even as a sliver of guilt seems to claw at my chest that I held her down that way, I can't help but feel like it was meant to happen. It was erotic and intimate and fucking hot as hell, and she said she wanted it rough, so I gave it my all.

And I get the feeling it will go down like that again.

We're both quietly processing afterward, and I get up to grab a washcloth to clean the mess I made on her ass.

She hasn't moved, and there's something inherently sexy about her waiting for me to make the next move. It's almost as if she's waiting for permission to move. I don't really want to give it to her. I want her to stay right there while I take care of her, and then I want to slide into the bed beside her and lay with her until her alarm forces us apart in the morning.

What is this? What the fuck is this?

I'm not sure, but I know I never want it to end.

What a terrifying thought.

Even if she was somehow unable to untie herself from Brooks, we still have very separate lives to lead. I'm not quitting ball just like she's not quitting singing and acting.

But a normal relationship is hard enough. Tack on the time apart because of travel and seasons and tours and movie shoots, and I'm terrified that we're dead in the water.

But I will do what it takes to fight for us. Whatever that might look like.

When the alarm rings far too early at five in the morning again so Gregory can pick her up at six to deliver her to hair and make-up, she groans as she turns it off.

She shimmies around in the dark a little, and I'm half-asleep, so I'm not really sure what she's doing, but then I feel her warm hand as it slides down into my boxer briefs. She grips my cock, and whoa, hello, I'm awake.

I grunt as she starts to pump her fist, my cock quickly waking up to what she's doing as all the blood rushes to one spot.

She slides her hand down to cup my balls, the feeling out of this fucking world as she handles me. I feel like I'm going to nut all over the place when she pulls her hand away and climbs on top of me. She's completely naked as she sits down on my cock, and I slide into her warm, wet pussy that's open and waiting for me.

She grinds on top of me, and I reach up to feel her tits while she fucks me.

What a goddamn way to wake up.

I'll take one of these alarm clocks every morning.

It's the complete opposite of last night as she moves sweetly over me, yet somehow, it moves us to the same place. She lifts up and down over me, and I grip her hips as I drive into her lazily from beneath. She arches back, sticking her tits out, and even in the darkness of the room, her silhouette is enough of a visual to push me right into my climax. I spill into her, and her pussy tightens over me as she comes right along with me.

Her gentle, soft morning moans are nothing like the screaming orgasm she had last night, yet we both found the same sort of pleasure out of what we're doing. And it's all the different angles with her, all the different feelings and emotions, that tell me *this* is where I'm meant to be.

Forever.

"God, I love you," I murmur as her orgasm wanes, and she pushes up so I slip out of her.

"I love you more," she says softly, and she presses a kiss to my neck.

"Wake me up like that every day, okay?" I request.

She giggles. "Deal. Every day I can."

I wish that equaled far more days than it actually does.

She heads out bright and early, which means I'm awake with little to do until the rest of the world wakes, too.

I do a few maintenance things around the house—fixing bulbs, replacing air filters, hanging some Christmas lights outside since it's tradition, that sort of shit, and I can't help but think I want to move out of this place. I want something bigger, with more privacy, but I never really needed it until I met Alexis. And she would never ask me to get a bigger house for her, but if she's going to be coming and going more regularly, she deserves a sprawling place meant for more than a single dude renting a house until he's sure where he's going to land.

I want to land wherever she is, though I'm tied to Vegas and the Heat for two more years. I could retire early and forfeit the rest of my check, but I don't want to do that. I *want* to play, and even though I want to give up everything for her, I know that's not what she'd want for me.

Just as I don't want her to give up her career for me…unless it means she gets away from her controlling father and fake fiancé.

I push those thoughts out of my head as I carry the ladder back to the garage, and then I call my mother.

"Hey baby boy," she answers.

"I'm thinking about coming to visit next week. Will you be around?"

"Actually, no. I'll be up at Anna's watching the boys."

"Watching the boys?" I repeat.

"She's going to Vegas to look at houses with Rush," she says softly.

"She…she is?"

"Yeah. And if she moves there, well, I suppose I'll probably move there, too," she says.

I love the idea of my mother being closer geographically.

"I'll find you a place, Mom. Is she moving *in* with Rush?" I ask.

"No, no. She's looking for a place for her and the boys, and Rush is helping her."

"I told her I'd help her," I protest. Hell, I told her I'd buy her a place.

"I know you did, and that was really kind of you. I think she just wants to start over, and she wants Rush involved in the process."

I guess I get that. It's kind of like how I'd want Alexis involved if I were to start looking, a thought that just barely entered into my subconscious a few hours ago.

"Can I come see you and the boys then? Maybe help out a little?" I ask.

"Of course."

I can't ignore the fact that Anna's place is only an hour from Alexis's, and if I'm an hour away, there's a better chance we'll find a way to see each other.

What I told Alexis was true. I'm not giving her up—no matter what. But the secrets, lies, and sneaking around are already getting tiresome, and we've just barely gotten off the ground.

I don't know how the fuck we're going to manage to keep doing this for the next few months, or year…or *years*. I don't know how long the merger will take and what other stipulations her father will draft up.

I'll fight because I'm in this thing with her.

I'll even fight the next battle that I never saw coming.

Chapter 17
Danny

I'm minding my own business when the doorbell rings, and I absentmindedly head over to see who's bothering me now with the smallest sliver of hope that it's Alexis back to surprise me even though I know how unlikely that is.

And when I open it, my father stands in front of me again—for the second time in as many days.

"What the fuck do you want now?" I demand.

I'm about to shut the door in his face when his mouth curls up into a smile—the kind that scares the fuck out of me. He's up to something, and it's not going to be good.

"I have something you might want to see," he says, pulling his phone out of his pocket. "But you should invite me in since you probably don't want me to play this video I have out here on your front porch for all the neighbors to see."

I roll my eyes and sigh, but then I open the door a little wider to allow him to walk in despite my better judgment telling me not to.

He hits play on his phone when the door closes behind him, and I hear my own voice as my eyes fall onto Alexis and myself in my bed. It takes all of a whole second for me to realize this was from last night.

"*Leave Brooks publicly. Be with me…publicly. Stop the charade. Stop the fake relationship—*" I'm saying in the video.

"What the fuck is this?" I ask, but I know full well what the fuck this is, and I know what she says next, and I know what *happens* next, too.

"You've been quite the little rabbit over here," he says snidely. "Last night *and* this morning?"

"Excuse me? What I do in my bedroom is nobody's business but mine." I clench my fists at my side as my body goes right into fight mode.

"I *knew* something was going on with you and that singer, and here's the evidence." He fast forwards the video until he gets to the good stuff. "Eye for an eye. You caught me, and now I've caught you."

The *one* saving grace is that when I moved over the top of her, you can't see her face. In fact, you can't see much of anything except for my backside, which is largely covered with clothes. So yeah, it's technically a sex tape, but the woman being fucked isn't all that visible once we actually start having sex.

The damage is done, though. It doesn't matter if she can be seen or not. The audio is clear, and the fact that I'm dominating her while holding her down is also clear.

And I can identify her easily in the part of the recording where we're laying on my bed having a heartfelt, honest conversation like we should be able to do in the privacy of my own fucking home. My own fucking *bed*.

My chest swirls with fear as I stare at the screen. "What the fuck is wrong with you?" I yell, slapping the phone out of his hand as it all comes together in my brain. He asked to use the bathroom yesterday. Brad called. I stepped outside, and this asshole was walking down the stairs when I stepped back inside.

He set me up. He planted a camera in my bedroom that I never even saw, and Alexis and I talked openly and honestly before I fucked her hard last night, and then she made love to me this morning.

"Don't worry," he says, leaving the phone on the floor. "The *scandalous sex tape* is all backed up to the cloud. You sure wouldn't want that leaking out now, would you? I mean, the conversation you had where you admitted she's faking with the other guy and you two are sneaking around was golden enough, but then I was lucky enough to catch the rest…"

"You're my *father*. How the fuck could you do this to me?" I scream at him.

"Am I? Because just yesterday, you said I'm dead to you and that you don't have a father. Pick a side, Daniel. Either I am or I'm not."

I stare at him for a beat as I try to figure out what to do, but I'm at a total loss here. The only thing I can feel is the hot rage coursing through my veins. My fists clench involuntarily at my sides again. "You do realize that what you've done is a crime, right? I could have you arrested."

"You won't," he says, and he's got a whole lot of confidence for a criminal who's the fucking scum of the earth. "Because if you did, then your little secret becomes public knowledge."

He's right. I can't turn him in because he's got the proof.

I have to protect Alexis. Whatever it takes, I have to protect her.

"Besides," he continues. "You know deep down that you and I are cut from the same cloth, Danny boy."

I hate him. I hate that I share blood with this man. I hate that he's any part of my life at all.

My fists clench again, and they're itching, *burning* to reach out and connect with his ugly face.

I rein it in. Hitting him now would feel good for a minute, but then I'd be setting myself up for something far worse. At least that common sense slides through my brain.

"What do you want from me?" I whisper.

"Well, the money we discussed yesterday would be a good start."

"A good start?" I repeat, terrified of what his next words might be.

"Yes, a good start. I'll need you to cover Olivia's gift, but I think the wife and I could also use a little nest egg, you know? Maybe a nice vacation somewhere. Oh, and of course, I'll need you to publicly acknowledge your wonderful father. Make me look like the good dad I am to the media. Make it look like you chose to be part of my life again."

"I would *never* choose you," I spit at him.

"Then I suppose I'll have to reveal what I know to the world."

"You wouldn't," I hiss.

"Watch me," he hisses right back.

I'm silent a beat as I consider that. He would. I really think he would.

"Why would you do this to me? Is it really about the money?" I ask.

He shakes his head as he presses his lips together, and his eyes are hard when they fall onto me. "You ruined my life."

"Excuse me?"

"You walked in on something you didn't understand, and you fucked with the balance of everything. You ruined my marriage. You ruined my family. You ruined everything. Your mother couldn't stay with me when she felt like she had to support *you*, so she kicked me out."

On Deck

"That's not how it happened," I protest. He *chose* his other family.

"You don't think so?" he demands. "You were seven, kid. You didn't have the first clue about what really happened back then. I'll take the first payment to cover the car by the end of the day today. I want to get her something real nice, so let's start at fifty-K and go from there, shall we? If it's not wired to this account by the close of business today, I'll send my video straight to the media." He hands me a card with an account number and routing number on it, and then he turns to leave.

"I fucking hate you," I say to his backside. "And just to be clear, we are *not* cut from the same cloth. I'd never do something like this to another person, let alone my own *son*."

He walks out the door, and I hold the card between my fingertips as I debate what the fuck I'm supposed to do next.

Chapter 18
Alexis

They say ignorance is bliss, and I'm blissfully ignorant as I text Danny after filming is done for the day.

Tomorrow is my last day filming here on location in Vegas, and then we will return to Los Angeles to film there starting Monday. I'll be back home with my dad. I won't get to come to Danny's house every night after the shoot to decompress and destress.

We'll be back to hiding this secret from a distance, and even though I believe in us, that doesn't make any of this any easier.

He'll have to watch as the wedding approaches. Tomorrow is the first of December, which means we're only two weeks away from this sham of a marriage becoming my new reality, and I know, I just *know* that my father will have the wedding splashed all over the media the minute I arrive back home.

The thought is heavy on my mind as Gregory pulls into Danny's driveway.

I want to show Danny how much I love him. I want to prove to him that he's it for me, that this wedding is only for my brand. But I have no idea how.

It feels like too much pressure. Tonight is our last night together. I have to leave for LA tomorrow after filming wraps, and I don't know when we'll see each other again.

I've built tonight up way too big in my mind to meet expectations, but that's what I do. I always build things up bigger than they are. Hopefully history will repeat itself in this case, and things won't be as dramatic as I think they are.

"I'll pick you up tomorrow at six unless we hear otherwise from the studio," Gregory tells me, and I thank him with shaking hands before I get out of the car. I head toward the front door and fall into Danny's waiting arms when he holds the door open for me.

He closes the door behind me, and he feels...stiff.

Something is wrong, and I get it. It all feels wrong to me, too.

"Are you okay?" I ask, my face buried in his chest.

He tightens his grip around me. "No."

"I'm not, either. How are we going to do this? How do I leave and go marry another man in two weeks?"

He doesn't respond, and an alarm rings in my head.

Why isn't he responding?

"Danny?" I ask softly.

He heaves out a long, heavy breath, and then he reaches down into his pocket.

I take a step back from him, my eyes on his hand before he opens it.

"I, uh...I have something I need to tell you."

My brows draw together. "What is it?"

He clears his throat, obviously nervous to tell me whatever it is.

"What's in your hand?" I ask, the alarm ringing louder in my head as fear grips its icy claws into my chest.

He opens his hand, holding what looks like a tiny video camera.

The crease between my brows deepens in confusion. "What is that?"

"A recording device, like a nanny cam."

"Why do you have it?" I ask. Fear pounds between my ears, a loud, constant thunder.

He averts his eyes to the ground. "My father...he planted it in my bedroom."

"He *what*?" I practically yell. "Wait...when?"

"Yesterday morning." His eyes won't meet mine as he says the words.

I press my lips together as my heart races. My first thought is the sex we had last night where he completely obliterated my body and my mind.

My second thought is the sex we had this morning.

And my third thought is...what the hell did we say to each other last night?

I was exhausted—emotionally spent after a hard day on set, wanting to be there for Danny because his father showed up out of the blue. He told me not to marry Brooks. We definitely talked about how this is all a sham and how I should be with him instead.

Oh my God.

As if the fact that his father *videotaped* us having sex wasn't bad enough, he also caught our very private conversation?

"Why the hell would he do that?" I demand quietly.

"He wants money." His voice is defeated.

"How much? I'll buy the damn video from him. Better yet, call the police! This must be a felony or something, right?" I reach into my back pocket and pull my phone out to make the call, but he shakes his head and takes the phone gently from my grasp.

"If we go to the police, that video becomes evidence."

"Have you...have you seen it?" I ask.

He closes his eyes and nods.

Shame fills me. I'm "cheating" on my "fiancé," and Danny's father took full advantage of that. He never knew when he planted that camera the absolute gold mine he was about to stumble upon, but he got pretty damn lucky.

"Are there more?" I ask.

His brows dip. "More what? Videos?"

"Cameras." I glance all around me, suddenly feeling scared to even be here at all.

He shakes his head. "I don't know. I spent the day looking around for more, but he got everything he wanted last night."

"What kind of sick person—" I cut myself off before I say more.

This is his father, and I don't want Danny to feel like he's *anything* like that man. But I'm not sure how to approach any of this.

"Let's ask Gregory what to do. He's here to protect me, and—"

He shakes his head. "I don't think we should tell anyone, Alexis. I already paid him what he wanted, so maybe this all goes away now."

"You gave him money?" I ask.

"I didn't have any other choice. He told me he'd release the tape if I didn't put fifty grand in his private account by the close of business today. So I did what I had to do," he says sullenly.

My stomach twists violently, and I feel like I'm going to be sick.

I can't believe any of this right now.

"And you think that's it?" I ask. "Fifty grand and he'll keep quiet?"

He lifts a shoulder. "I don't know. No, not really. I don't think that's it. But what other choice did I have?"

"Let's talk to Gregory," I beg as tears start to pinch behind my eyes. "He'll know what to do."

He shakes his head. "Let me handle him. I don't want to drag anyone else into this mess." He says the words with finality, and it feels like there's no more arguing.

"I'm scared, Danny."

He grabs me into his arms again. "I am, too, Lex. But we've made it to here. We'll figure this out, too."

"What if we don't? What if he releases that tape? It'll ruin everything I've worked for. My image will be destroyed. My brand decimated. My reputation wrecked. And the merger my dad wants so badly…" I trail off as I start to cry in earnest.

"I won't let that happen," he says fiercely.

"What are you going to do? Is all this even worth it?" I ask through the tears.

He pulls back and his eyes fall to mine, and for the first time, I see my own fears reflected back at me. "Of course it's worth it," he says quietly.

And then he hauls me up into his arms and carries me up to his room, where he gently rubs my back until I stop crying.

But just because the tears stop doesn't mean I'm any less scared about what the future holds for us.

Chapter 19
Danny

It probably goes without saying, but we didn't screw last night. We both lay awake staring at the ceiling instead, not exchanging a single word as we each found ourselves lost in our own thoughts.

She's probably thinking over the words she voiced to me before: *Is all this even worth it?*

Or maybe she's scared to be here—scared that her privacy will be violated again. Scared that we *both* will be violated again. I'm scared of that, too. I'm scared of what my father could do to us. I'm scared of what he's holding over us.

I'm scared he's going to spell the impending end for us, and the fear is so real and tangible that my stomach twists.

The thought that I should move sooner than later darts through my mind. Maybe *I* need some personal security, too—someone to keep assholes like my father out of my life and away from my front door.

And I, of course, allowed her words to turn over in my mind as they grew tentacles that latched onto every good feeling I have about us.

My dad ruined my life when he cheated on my mother. Was that not enough? He has to do it again?

According to him, though, I'm the one who ruined *his* life.

Clearly he's held onto that grudge for the last twenty years, and now here we are, coming off a World Series win just a month ago as I embark on this secret affair with the woman beside me, one of the most powerful women in the world.

She deserves better than me, but I deserve better than the father I was born to.

I hate that it's my fault we're here.

I'm sure she'd tell me it *isn't* my fault, that I'm not to blame, that I'm not anything like him.

Except…maybe I am.

As I lie awake, I'm searching for ways to ruin him. I could approach his wife and ruin his life…again. I could kick his ass with my bare fucking hands.

There are any number of approaches I could take, and as all the possibilities dart through my mind, I'm ultimately not sure which would cause the least amount of damage to the woman next to me.

And that's my top priority here. I refuse to let this hurt her, which is why I told her about it in the first place.

I could tell Gregory. That's certainly an option.

But I feel like I bought some time by paying off the first debt. I'm hopeful it's enough to keep him off my back for a little while anyway, though I wouldn't put it past him to show up at my door in the morning telling me it's not enough.

As it turns out, that's precisely what happens.

Alexis and I share a difficult goodbye as she tells me she's catching a flight back to Los Angeles tonight.

On Deck

"I'm visiting my mom next week, and she'll be staying with my sister in Dana Point. I won't be far. Maybe we can meet up."

She nods and clings to me as we both feel the force of the impending separation. I don't know what will change from now until the next time I see her.

Maybe things won't work between us, and we won't get to see each other before her wedding. What if she's married to someone else the next time I hold her in my arms?

The thought claws and tears at my heart. I've never felt pain like this, and as I press my lips to hers, I feel the sting of heat behind my own eyes as the fears start to push their way to the surface.

She heads out at six with a promise not to breathe a word about any of this to anyone, including Gregory, and the man who donated sperm to my mother in order to give me life shows up at my door around ten once again, like horrible fucking clockwork.

"Thanks for the payment," he says as he stands on my front porch, looking like the goddamn rat he is.

"You're welcome. Now get the fuck out."

He offers one of those smiles that makes me feel sick to my stomach. "Thanks for the cash, but where's the public show of how close we are now?"

"Fuck off with that shit. I will *never* do that."

"Do you really want to test me? I'd be happy to release that tape." He's so casual about it, so uncaring, that it makes my skin crawl.

It also makes me wonder when this will ever end.

Maybe Alexis is right. Maybe we need to get Gregory involved. Or *someone*. I just have no idea who.

"I'm going to visit my mother and my nephews. Give me some time. I'll be back next week, and we can talk then," I mutter.

"Fifty-K more or I go to the media. And invite your father inside the damn house. Didn't anybody ever teach you any manners?"

I laugh snidely. "Yeah. My mother told me not to talk to strangers and especially not to invite them into my home."

"I'm not a stranger." He pushes forcefully to get into my home, but I keep my foot braced behind the door.

"You're not anybody I know, that's for damn sure. Get the fuck out of here."

"Cut the check first," he demands.

"Fine." I slam the door in his face and lock it for good measure, and then I head up to grab my phone because I don't even have a fucking checkbook. I return to my front door and make the same wire transfer as yesterday as I show it to him. "Now leave me the fuck alone."

"You have one week," he says, and then he spins around to leave.

"I fucking hate you," I say to his retreating back.

He doesn't even flinch, and that's when I realize the depth of the psychopath I'm dealing with here.

Chapter 20
Alexis

I'm having a hard time staying in character today as the things Danny told me last night roll over in my mind.

I promised not to say a word to anyone, and Leila keeps asking me if everything's okay. I've flubbed my lines over and over today, missed my cues, and generally cost the entire production nearly a full day of filming. Luckily, we only had a little bit left to film here, and somehow I manage to get through it.

And then I find myself on a plane with Gregory, who leans over beside me. "Is everything okay, ma'am?"

I press my lips together and stare out the window.

He probably thinks I'm just being a little dramatic about leaving Danny. He has no idea the depth of what's going on in my mind, and I truly do feel like he'd have some insight into how to deal with this.

But I promised Danny I'd keep quiet, so against my better judgment, I don't say a word.

For now.

But when does this thing with his dad end?

How far will he push us? Until we break? And *why* would he do that to his own son?

It's something so incomprehensible to me, yet as I look at my own situation…is it really all that different?

Both our dads are taking what they want from us. They're manipulating us to get their way. They're using us for our successes. For our money. For whatever else they want.

And none of it is right.

In fact, all it's doing is pushing us closer together. It's giving us one more thing to bond over. It's giving us one more thing in common…no matter how sick and twisted that is.

I feel sick to my stomach that someone has a *sex tape* of us. This has the potential to ruin me. To ruin my career. To ruin everything I've built for the last ten years.

But even so, even with all that heaviness and fear…I find myself wanting to turn into Danny. I'm not running away. Instead, I want to run *to* him.

I can't. I have to get home.

But more than anything, I wish I could stay with him so we could figure things out.

I'm quiet the entire short flight, and just before we get off the plane, I turn to Gregory as I slip my sunglasses on. "Can you help me avoid the media in the airport? I just…I don't have it in me right now."

He nods. "Of course."

The flight attendant lets us off the plane first, and he takes me through the terminal with an arm around my shoulders. I keep my head down and sunglasses on, avoiding eye contact with anyone who wants something from me this evening because right now, I have nothing left to give of myself.

It's all back in Vegas with Danny.

On Deck

When I met him, I never had the first inclination that life would become so complicated so quickly. But I never had the first inclination about how much it would be worth it either.

I feel very much alone as Gregory ushers me to the car parked by the private terminal. As we slip into the car, I pull out my phone to text Danny to let him know I've landed.

I see I have a missed call from Brooks, and he left a voicemail, so before I text Danny, I take a quick listen.

"Alexis, sorry to leave this via voice message, but it's your father. He was having trouble catching his breath. He was coughing and wheezing, so I took him back to the ER. We just arrived. I, uh…I just thought you should know."

My heart sinks as my chest tightens.

"Gregory?" I ask softly.

"Ma'am?"

"Can you take me to Cedars Sinai instead of home?"

"Is everything all right?" he asks.

"My dad is at the ER again. Coughing, wheezing, shortness of breath."

"I'm sorry, Alexis. Yes, of course," he says.

I dial Brooks back.

"Hello," he answers.

"Is he okay?" My voice sounds panicked even to myself.

"He was just taken back, and he's getting checked out, so he's in the right place. Have you landed?"

"Yes. We're on our way to the hospital. I'm glad you were there with him."

"He's like a father to me, too, Alexis," he says quietly, and he's the type of person who rarely shows emotion, so it feels significant that he said that.

And he *will* be his father, too—father-in-law, anyway, two weeks from today.

The thought hits me in a different place, and the result is pure confusion.

It's not what I want...and yet, as I face my father being back in the hospital and as I see once again how short life is, I can't help but feel like I'm doing the right thing by marrying Brooks.

It's the right thing for my dad. It's the right thing for Brooks.

And as for me, well...maybe I'm putting off my happy ending by a year or so, and maybe those are terms my dad and I will hammer out over the next few days.

Or maybe I'll lose him here tonight and never get those answers.

The thought pulses new fears inside me while digging up the ones I put to rest the last time he was in here.

Gregory parks at the back entrance like last time and ushers me inside. I know where to go this time, familiar with it since it wasn't all that long ago I was here.

A nurse spots me and immediately recognizes me. "Your father is this way," she says, and Gregory retreats back outside. I think about telling him to come with me, but I know I need to face this alone.

The nurse opens the door to my father's private room in the ER, and he looks a little older than when I saw him less than a week ago. He's got another oxygen tube under his nose, and apart from seeming a little distressed that he's back here, he seems okay.

"We can't keep meeting here like this," he quips, and I roll my eyes.

"Why are you here?"

"Apparently you were right. I was supposed to finish the whole bottle of meds, not stop once I felt better."

I roll my eyes. "Are you serious right now?"

He has the grace to look a little sheepish.

On Deck

"You scared the heck out of me, Daddy. I told you to take your medicine." I fold my arms across my chest and press my lips together.

"I know you did, and I just...got busy. I was fine until I wasn't."

"Clearly." I nod toward the bed he's lying in.

"Twice in a week, and I think I'm starting to learn something," he admits.

"What?"

He glances at the nurse, who's busy looking at his IV bag, and then she leaves the room for a moment.

"Life's short, and I need this merger done. I need you to go through with the wedding."

"I know. I've already agreed to it," I say.

"You did, but I get the feeling you're hiding things from me, and that didn't start until you met Danny Brewer." He gives me a pointed look, and my chest tightens that maybe he knows more than I give him credit for.

And that gives me the strangest feeling that Danny's dad isn't the only patriarch keeping eyes on things that are none of his business.

I can't help but circle back to one question, though.

Why?

Chapter 21
Danny

When the text from AJ comes through asking if I'm up for drinks tonight with him and Nick, I opt in for a change.

My girl just left, my father is blackmailing me, and it feels like my life is falling apart. Going out with some buddies and drinking my troubles away for the night sounds like exactly what I need right now.

I text Rush and Cooper on a whim, and as it turns out, they're both in, too.

It's just like old times with the five of us out on the town…except it's *nothing* like old times since Cooper has a kid, Rush is banging my sister, and I'm tied up with the world's most famous pop princess.

What the hell happened to us?

I swear to God, if Cooper shows up in a Hawaiian shirt and starts telling Dad jokes, I may lose it.

I've already lost so much of myself that I'm starting to feel unsure of who I even am anymore.

Without Alexis here, I feel myself falling apart. It's the off-season, and I always go through a bit of a mourning period after every season. It felt like it took a little longer to get here since we were busy celebrating our World Series win, but I think that's where I'm finding myself tonight.

Or maybe it's my father's threats and her being back in Los Angeles just crashing into my emotions. Whatever it is, I don't like what I feel, and what better way to get rid of that than *not* feeling it at all?

With that in mind, I hit my vape a few times while I wait for a car to drag me over to Skip's to meet the boys. The THC hits my bloodstream before the car arrives, and I'm already feeling a calming sensation before I even leave my house.

This was what I needed.

When I arrive, I spot Cooper first. He's laughing, and my eyes slide to Rush beside him, who surely said something to make him laugh the way he is. AJ is there, too, and I slip into the booth next to him. A full beer sits in front of me, and I grab it and take a sip.

"That's Nick's," AJ says, and I shrug.

"Looks like it's mine now." I wave Kelly over and tap my drink when she shows up. "I stole Nick's, and it's a little light for me. Can you bring another one of these plus a whiskey for me?"

She nods, and I get to work on the light beer.

Nick returns from his trip, presumably to the restroom, and he glares at me as I finish his drink.

I hold up both hands. "Sorry. In my defense, it was full, and I was thirsty."

"Dick," Nick mutters, and I laugh.

On Deck

The laughter feels good. It feels like it's been far too long since I really and truly laughed, though I'm sure Alexis and I were laughing over some dumb shit just the other day.

Before things got so damn heavy.

Before the weight started crushing my chest.

I put it out of my mind for now. I have to. I'm out with friends, and nothing changes anyway, even if I wasn't.

"How was everyone's Thanksgiving?" Cooper asks.

Everyone shares a little about how theirs went, and I glance at Rush before he pipes up.

He knows this thing with Alexis is supposed to be secret, but liquor makes loose lips sometimes.

"Mine was nice. I spent time with the woman I've been seeing and her family," he says.

"This thing with this mystery woman…it's getting pretty serious, yeah?" AJ asks.

Rush presses his lips together and bobs his head up and down a little. "Yep, it is. She's near LA now and looking to move here to Vegas."

Cooper's brows shoot up, and I realize nobody here knows that Rush is with *my sister*. But if he's not sharing my secret, I won't share his, either.

"Wow, that's big news," Cooper says.

"Yeah," he murmurs. He shifts his attention to me. "How 'bout you?"

"It was good. Spent time with my family," I say a little absently. I leave out the part that I also spent time with my girlfriend—and, of course, with Rush.

I want to talk to him about my sister moving here and what it all means, but I don't want to do it in front of everyone else. And for a beat, I even consider confiding in him about what's been going on. I feel like I can trust him, and we've gotten pretty close over the last year.

But considering how close he is with my sister, I'm not sure he's the right person to talk to.

I glance over at Cooper, who's eyeing me curiously—as if he already suspects something. And I know if there's one dude at this table I can trust with my life, it's Cooper Noah.

Even if he tells Gabby.

I guess at this point…I trust her, too.

Eventually, AJ and Nick saunter out of the booth and hit the prowl, leaving Rush, Coop, and me alone.

"So this mystery woman," Cooper begins, pinning Rush with a look.

Rush nods. "It's Danny's sister."

"Ah. And you're okay with this?" He turns to me.

I shrug. "Not my place to tell either of them who they can or can't see."

"Wow," Cooper breathes. "Never thought I'd see the day."

"Never thought you'd see what day?" I ask.

"The day where you were so taken with somebody that you're actually okay with a teammate being with your sister." He gives me a pointed look.

"Apparently, they were secretly seeing each other for quite some time, scared to tell me what they'd been doing. And you know what?" I take a quick sip of whiskey. "Everyone deserves a little slice of happiness, and if that's what they give to each other, then good for them."

"Wow, man. You know what that tells me?" Cooper asks.

I glance up at him.

"That you're in deep with AB." He picks up his beer.

"Oh, he's in deep. *Balls* deep," Rush says snidely, and I can't help but laugh at that.

But that laugh is quickly followed by a sigh when I remember just how deep I actually find myself. "Yeah, I'm in deep all right."

"Why all the heaviness, then?" Cooper asks, sharp as always.

I glance between the two men on the other side of the table, and I realize telling Alexis that we need to keep this quiet was the wrong call. She *should* get advice from Gregory. And I should get advice from my friends.

Maybe a little stoned paired with a little drunk isn't the exact formula for going about that, yet here I am.

I lean in a little closer to my friends even though the music is loud enough in here that nobody will overhear me.

"My dad has something on us. He planted a camera and caught a private conversation, among *other things*, and now he's blackmailing me for money and plans to expose us if I don't pay up."

"What other things?" Rush asks at the same time Cooper says, "Jesus Christ. Are you serious?"

I give Rush a pointed look. "The same things I walked in on my father doing to another woman when I was seven. He claims me telling my mother about that whole thing ruined his life, and this is apparently some twisted act of revenge."

"Was the conversation damning?" Cooper asks.

I nod. "It spelled out in no uncertain terms what we mean to each other. And, uh…what *other* relationships *don't* mean."

"That's criminal, isn't it?" Rush asks.

I nod as my brows rise. "You bet your ass it is. But turning him in means turning that tape in, which means I can't protect *her*."

They both stare at me as if they're not quite sure what to say and honestly…I'm not quite sure, either.

"How much have you paid him?" Cooper asks.

"A hundred grand so far, but he also wants me to publicly acknowledge that we've mended our relationship and that he's a great father," I admit. "Which…I can't even think about it without feeling like I'm going to vomit."

"Wow," Cooper breathes. "So what are you going to do? Keep paying him out?"

"What's my other choice?" I ask.

Cooper shakes his head a little as he processes it all, but Rush jumps right in with an answer.

"If he found shit on you…you find shit right back on him." He says it like I'm stupid for not considering that myself—and maybe I am.

Maybe he's right.

"You know anybody who could do that kind of thing for me?" I ask.

Cooper remains silent, but Rush nods. "I have a cousin who's a private investigator. I'd be happy to hook you up."

Well, you learn something new every day about your friends, I guess.

"Talk to him for me, would you?" I ask. "See if he has room in his schedule for me."

"She," he says pointedly.

"She?"

He nods. "She. Chloe. And she's incredible at what she does."

"Okay, then. Hook us up as soon as you can."

He pulls his phone out of his pocket and sends a text. "She'll be in touch with you."

"Thanks, man," I say. And now, I suppose…we wait.

Chapter 22
Danny

I order another whiskey, and three ladies approach our table.

The problem is that my vision is starting to blur. In the past, that wouldn't have been a bad thing. Whoever slid in beside me would've been the girl I went home with.

Tonight, however, that isn't in the cards.

"Danny Brewer," the woman says. She's blonde and vaguely familiar, but I'm just not in the mood for this. I turn to look at her, and she's shaking her head with disappointment. "You don't remember me, do you?"

I squint at her a little, and something about animal print comes to mind.

A leopard, maybe? She's wearing a leopard print dress right now, and it's calling up some hazy memory like I've seen that dress before.

On my bedroom floor.

Long fingernails. Something about round three.

"Erica," she says. "We hooked up last March. You didn't remember my name when you asked me to leave your place."

"Right, Erica!" I say, feigning enthusiasm. "Of course I remember—both you *and* your name," I lie.

I remember being wasted, but most of the night with Erica is shot completely from my memory at this point.

"You don't have to lie, but I *am* still ready for round three." She offers a flirtatious smile at me.

Her friend across the table next to Rush yells, "Smile!"

We both glance over at her out of pure habit when someone yells such a word, but I don't smile.

"Try again," she says, and Erica leans in beside me with her cheek against mine as she cheeses it up for the camera.

Well, that's one photo that will likely end up all over the tabloids by morning.

Last week, I was photographed out with Kit Davenport, and this week, it's Erica the Leopard.

I think for just a beat what would happen if I *did* take Erica up on her offer.

In some ways, I want it to feel like it's my right. I want to feel like it'd be evening the score with Alexis since she's about to *marry* some other dude.

But it doesn't feel that way at all. Instead, it feels like it would be a terrible mistake...one I refuse to make since I have everything I've ever wanted with Alexis.

Still, her words about whether it's all worth it pierce through my skull for the millionth time since she spoke the concern.

I assured her it *is* worth it...but how can I be sure when there's so goddamn much at stake? Between her marriage, and her father's company, and her fucking brand, and her reputation...it's a whole lot for her to lose by being paired with somebody like me.

The only thing I have to lose in all this is myself. My heart.

Because if there's one thing I'm sure of at this point, it's that she owns all of it.

"So where are we at on that round three?" Erica asks, sliding one of those long fingernails down my bicep.

"I had a fun night with you back in March, Erica," I say quietly, trying my best to let her down gently. "But I'm just not in the right place for round three tonight."

"Tonight?" she says, clearly grabbing onto some false hope I certainly didn't mean to give her. "So maybe another night, then?"

"I'm sorry," I say quietly.

She purses her lips for a beat. "You're going to regret this," she hisses at me.

Is there a jungle cat that hisses?

I'm not sure why *that* is the thought that bears down on me, but it is. "I'm afraid I won't."

I thought she would've gotten the message loud and clear when I kicked her out without remembering her name, but she didn't. And now here we are, another mark stacked against us on the side that's clearly winning the race.

I excuse myself to the restroom and detour for the front door on my way. I head outside and slip around the side of the building where it's quiet, and I call Alexis.

She doesn't pick up. I leave a voicemail.

"Hey. I went out with my buddies tonight, and this girl I was with back before we met hit on me. I wanted to let you know her friend snapped our photo together, and I don't doubt it'll be all over social media by morning. Anyway, I hope you had a good flight. I miss you and wish we were still together at the Beverly Wilshire or my place. I wish we could rewind a few days before my father showed up to throw a wrench into things. I wish a lot of things, but most of all, I wish you were still here. Well...I guess I'll talk to you soon. Bye."

I end the call, and when I turn to go back inside, I see Erica standing at the edge of the building watching me.

"Who'd you just call?" she asks.

"I'm sorry, but I don't owe you an answer to that." My voice is hard and firm, and I start walking around her to head back inside to my friends when she starts yelling.

"No! Danny, stop it!"

My brows dip as I take a step back from her. "What are you doing?"

"I said no!" she yells.

"What the fuck are you doing?" I hiss.

She offers me a wicked smile. "I told you you'd regret telling me no."

"So, what, you're making it look like I'm assaulting you?"

She shrugs. "I guess I am." She raises her voice. "No means no!"

"What's going on back here?" a male voice demands.

I close my eyes and shake my head. "I didn't fucking touch her," I say to the bouncer, who moves in behind her.

He's eyeing me warily, and he glances up and nods at a camera. "That should tell us everything. Both of you, back to the offices now."

What the actual fuck. Is he serious right now?

"I was literally making a call, and she followed me out here," I protest.

"The footage from the camera up there will let us know who's telling the truth. We'll take a look and determine whether we need to call the police," he says.

"Call them on her," I say, and I hear the exhaustion in my own voice. "Falsely accusing someone of a felony is a crime."

Her brows dip as she looks from me back to the bouncer. We both know what we're going to see on that tape.

On Deck

She sighs. "Ugh. Fine. He didn't touch me." She rolls her eyes and purses her lips before she spins on her heel and walks back into the bar.

"Thank you," I say to the bouncer.

"I know you, man. You've been around here a lot, and you've always been respectful. I didn't believe it for a second, but I had to let her feel that support, too."

"You're a good man. I'll hook you up with some tickets next season, okay?" I offer.

"No need," he says. "Coop already gave me the hook-up, and any friend of his is a friend of mine."

I laugh. "Glad to have people like you cheering us on."

I reserve a Lyft, head back inside to say goodbye to my friends, and decide to call it a night.

Chapter 23
Alexis

Well, he made quick work of that.

I'm scrolling my phone as it starts to ring with a call from Danny. As much as I want to take the call, I'm still sitting in the ER with my father, so I send the call to voicemail even as I look at the photo that was just posted.

It's him with some girl in a leopard print dress, and they're both smiling. Danny's eyes look glassy, and she looks like she's ready to strip that animal print right off for him. Or maybe she looks sort of like she already has done that with him before.

The thought of all the women he's been with darts through my mind. He can have his pick, and he chose me. And I can have my pick, too—and it appears like I'm choosing Brooks when I'm not.

I hate this. I hate everything about it.

But then I glance up at my father and see the oxygen still helping him breathe as he closes his eyes and rests, and a surge of confusion plows through me.

What if I'm too late? What if Danny doesn't want to deal with this whole mess we're in as I prepare to marry Brooks? What if he doesn't want to pay off his father to protect me?

What if it's just too complicated and we can't make it past all this?

I wouldn't blame him if he ran.

I want to believe we can beat all this. I want to believe we *will*.

But there's just so much in our way that it's getting harder and harder to believe it.

I send him a text after he leaves the voicemail.

Me: *I can't listen to your message right now. When I landed, I got word my dad was back in the hospital. He didn't take the rest of his meds. [eyeroll emoji] He'll be fine, but I'm sitting with him now. Love you.*

I wait for his reply, but it doesn't come. It doesn't even look like he's read my message yet.

I set my phone aside, tired of looking at photos of him with other women when it should be me.

Just two weeks, and then it'll be the wedding.

And I will make sure that as soon as the merger goes through, I can get out of this thing.

I'm curious how all that will work, though—considering my father isn't going to want it to look like we only got married for the merger...even if that's the truth.

I'm curious how long he'll want us to stay married. I'm curious how it'll look if I bow out immediately and what that will do to my brand, not to mention what it'll do to Brooks's reputation, too, and what it'll do to the business.

What if my dad was lying when he said we could get divorced later?

What if he expects me to stay with Brooks for an extended period of time?

What, exactly, have I agreed to?

On Deck

I feel a panic attack starting to edge its way in as I consider all these things, but I won't let this get the better of me.

I draw in a deep breath. I consider borrowing the oxygen under my dad's nose, but I know better.

I close my eyes and practice some deep breathing as I picture Danny's face.

It seems to be about the only thing that works to calm my thoughts these days. My therapist once told me to picture a safe place like a tranquil beach.

My safe place has become Danny Brewer.

The panic moves out as I breathe in and out and imagine him and me together.

When thoughts of his father and the tape creep in, I push them out as I think about how it feels when Danny's arms are around me. When thoughts of marrying Brooks start to take over, I force myself to feel Danny's lips on mine. When confusion over the future of my brand and my business begin to overwhelm me, I visualize how safe I feel when I'm with Danny.

Danny appears to be my answer for everything.

But my dad would tell me I'm asking the wrong questions.

He can't be my answer when I have to marry Brooks in two weeks.

And now that my dad is tied up here, it's more important than ever that I see through the wedding that should never happen.

At what price, though? The price of my own happiness. My own freedom. My own safety.

I wish it could be different. I wish I could have those things. I wish I could live a free and happy life where I make my own decisions.

But apparently when I was sixteen, I decided I didn't need those things, and now that I'm a grown woman…it's too late. I already signed those things away, and I'm starting to think that Danny deserves more than I can give him anyway.

"What are you thinking about, my darling girl?" my dad asks.

I glance up at him. I hadn't realized he was awake and watching me.

I clear my throat, about to unload some of the overwhelm I feel since I need some answers here when I realize…this isn't the time or the place.

I can't ask him how long he wants me to stay married to Brooks when he's in a hospital bed.

These are conversations that would be better next week when we're back home and talking about wedding plans.

"Nothing," I say softly. "Just worried about you." *And everything else.*

"No need to worry," he says. "I'll be fine. And I promise to finish my medication this time."

"I'll be there to make sure of it." I purse my lips, and he chuckles at the role reversal of the daughter taking care of the dad.

I just wish we were in a place where he could still take care of me, too—in the ways that matter to me.

Not in the ways that matter to him.

Chapter 24
Danny

I bang on the door, and my mom opens it a minute later. I practically fall into her arms.

I just saw her for Thanksgiving less than ten days ago, but it feels like a lifetime has passed since then.

I won't tell her about what my father has been doing to me since I last saw her. She's been through enough hell at the hands of that man. She doesn't need to take on the guilt I know she would take on if I admitted he recorded me having sex without my consent, and now he's using it to blackmail me.

"Whoa, Danny boy. You okay?" she asks, squeezing me tightly to her.

I let out a heavy sigh.

"Missing your girl already?" she asks knowingly as if that's the answer here. It's definitely part of it, but it's not the entire picture.

"I am," I say. I pull back out of her warm embrace and follow her inside.

"No bags?" she asks.

I shake my head. "I got a hotel in Long Beach. Figured the boys might want to go swimming and then I'd be out of your hair here."

"And also then maybe Alexis could swing down for a visit?" she guesses.

"There's always that possibility, though her father keeps her on a pretty tight leash. He's in the hospital right now, and she's marrying Brooks in less than two weeks, and it's...complicated."

"He's in the hospital?" she asks.

I nod. "He's likely getting released today. He'll be okay. Something with fluid in his lungs, and then he didn't finish out his medication."

She purses her lips and shakes her head. "I don't know him very well, but he sounds as stubborn as a donkey."

"I think the phrase is stubborn as a *mule*," I say dryly.

"Aren't they the same thing?" she asks. "A mule and a donkey, I mean."

I shake my head. "No. A mule is part-horse, part-donkey. A donkey is donkey-donkey."

"Ba-donkey donkey?" Leo asks, sauntering into the room.

"Hey, Leo," I say, grabbing my nephew into a hug as I lift him off his feet. He giggles, and I set him back down. He scampers out of the room, and my mom leans into me and lowers her voice.

"Either way, both donkeys and mules are a couple of asses," she jokes with the oldest, cheesiest joke in the books when it comes to donkeys and mules.

"How long have you been holding onto that one?" I ask.

"How'd you get to know so much about donkeys and mules?" she counters.

I shrug. "I thought it was common knowledge."

"Well it's not, and I'm not sure yet if Alexis's father is a donkey or a mule," she says, pursing her lips.

"Or just an ass," I mutter just as Lucas walks into the room.

"You said a bad word!" he yells at me, and I laugh.

"I say lots of them, but you definitely shouldn't," I tell him as I muss up his hair. He moves his head out of my reach and runs out of the room, too.

It already feels good being here, and I just walked in the door.

My mom treats me to some of the Kool-Aid she made for the boys and makes me a snack of grapes and cheese. It really doesn't feel so bad being here, getting taken care of by my mom.

I text Alexis after dinner when she takes the boys upstairs for their baths.

Me: *Is your dad out yet?*

Alexis: *He was released this afternoon. Doing much better.*

Me: *Any chance you can get away? I'm visiting my mom at my sister's place. Staying in Long Beach.*

Her answer doesn't come right away, and at first I assume it's because she's trying to figure out a way.

Disappointment lances through me when the response finally comes.

Alexis: *I wish I could. I'm sorry.*

Me: *I wish you could, too, but I understand.*

And that's where we leave it.

It feels like a wedge settling between us, and I hate it.

It's not going to get any easier once she marries Brooks. There will be so much more at stake when it comes to making sure nobody finds out about us.

But the cat's already out of the bag in terms of my inner circle. I trust everyone I've told, but then there's my father…the one person who knows that neither of us told.

And he's a loose cannon. I have no idea what his next move will be.

I have no reason to head back to the hotel yet since Alexis can't get out to meet me, so I stay put on my sister's couch. I wait for my mom as I watch sports highlights from today on ESPN, and when she comes back down, she sits beside me.

"You doing okay, DJ?" she asks.

"I'm doing as well as can be expected given the circumstances." I let out a heavy sigh.

"I just saw the announcement. I figured that's why you've been a little gloomy this evening."

My brows dip. "What announcement?"

"About Alexis and the wedding." She says it sort of like a question, and I still have no idea what she's talking about.

Clearly the look on my face expresses that confusion.

"There was an official announcement that she's marrying Brooks Donovan on December fifteenth at the San Ysidro Ranch."

"Oh," I say quietly.

I already knew all that, but I suppose the rest of the world didn't.

"That's ten days from tomorrow," she says quietly.

"I know."

"You're sure it's not real with him?" she asks.

"I'm sure it *is* real with me."

"I'm proud of you, you know," she says softly.

"For what?"

"For not running away from this. I can see how important this is to you, and I was worried the things that happened between your father and me when you were just a kid scared you off from wanting this for yourself," she says.

"It did," I admit. "But then I met the person I can't live without."

She reaches over and grabs my hand. "Then fight, Danny. Don't let her marry someone else."

"What choice do I have?"

She shrugs, and she rests her head on my shoulder. "I don't know, honey. But I love her for you, and I hate seeing you like this. I don't want you to run away scared because of the abandonment issues your father left you with."

I clear my throat. "He said something to me once that I keep thinking about." I don't mention that it's something he literally said to me a few days ago.

"What is it?" She straightens as she turns to listen with her brows drawn together.

"He said it was my fault our family broke up. He blamed me for ruining his life, for telling you. He said I didn't know what really happened, that you felt like you *had* to support me and couldn't stay with him because of what I discovered so you kicked him out. For me."

She clenches her jaw at my words, and her eyes turn hard. "He really said that?"

I press my lips together and nod.

"He made my life hell, Danny. Don't you believe for a second that I didn't kick him out because of his own actions. He made a fool of me. He ruined our family. But you know what you did?" She takes my chin between her fingertips. "You brave little boy, you gave us the truth. You gave us the family we deserved. You became the man of the house, and you grew up far sooner than you should've had to because *he* was a bad man. Don't you ever for a second think that you ruined a single thing. I thank God every single day that you were brave enough to tell me what you saw even though you didn't understand it."

"I knew it was wrong because of the way he reacted when I walked in. He told me not to tell you, but you raised me not to keep secrets. And now here I am…keeping a secret from the world. I'm a fucking hypocrite, Mom," I say, and I feel the weight of my own words.

"It's different," she says.

"How? She's with another man and I'm the other man. I'm no better than the woman I caught Dad on top of."

She flinches at my words, and I flinch when I say them.

"She's not married," she points out. "There aren't kids involved. She openly admitted she doesn't love him and she's only marrying him for business reasons. And you know what? I talked to her, Danny. I trust her. I believe her. I would never, *ever* encourage you to be with her if I didn't think she was being genuine with you."

I nod. "I know you wouldn't." We're both quiet a beat, and I think about retreating into my fears. I think about walking away from Alexis. I think about a lot of things…but ultimately, I know I can't.

I love her far too much to let her go.

And I think my mom may be right.

It's time to fight.

Chapter 25
Danny

I end up staying the night on the couch. The conversation with my mom was emotionally exhausting, and I didn't have the energy to drive for an hour to the hotel.

Plus, I had a couple of beers, and the couch is comfortable enough.

I didn't tell my mom about my dad last night despite the frank and honest conversation we had, and before I fell asleep, I thought about how telling her might be the right thing to do. It might give me the answers I'm looking for.

When I wake in the morning, it's because something feels…off. My eyes open slowly, and I find a four-year-old's blue eyes just inches from my face.

"Ah!" I yell, startled by the kid in my face as my own eyes pop open, and Leo bursts into giggles.

"You look funny when you sleep, Uncle Danny," he singsongs to me.

"Good morning to you, too, kid," I mutter as I sit up.

"Why are you sleeping on the couch?" he asks.

I shrug. "Fell asleep here last night."

"Gramma said you got a hotel, and maybe we can go swim at it after school."

I nod. "Well, that was the plan until you woke me up by staring at me."

He makes a pouty face and some whiney noise that my own children will *never* make, and then I remember something Anna said to me once about how we always have this idea of what we'll be like as parents before we have kids, and it all goes to shit once they're born.

And I freeze for a beat as I realize the thought I just had…

It's the first time I've ever really thought about having my own kids. I said in my head that my own children won't make that noise, as if I'm destined to actually have children someday.

I never thought of kids as a definite thing…until Alexis.

I suppose I never thought about a lot of things I'm starting to want out of my future until Alexis.

She's a game changer for me, and I need to do whatever I can to make sure she doesn't walk down that aisle toward Brooks in ten days.

But since I can't call her or see her, that's going to be a difficult feat.

"When can we see Awexis again?" Leo asks.

It's like the kid can read my goddamn mind, and that's a little terrifying.

"I'm not sure, buddy. But I'll definitely put in the request that you want to sing another song with her."

"Thanks, Uncle Danny."

"Leo!" We both hear my mother calling the kid, and he makes a face at me before he runs upstairs to see what she wants.

On Deck

My phone rings shortly after he heads up, and when I see it's Brad calling, I roll my eyes.

"You're lucky I was already awake because if I wasn't, I'd be spending my afternoon searching for a new agent."

"Funny jokes, big guy, but you might want to listen to *why* I'm calling before you start with the threats. We have a bit of a PR crisis."

"A PR crisis?" I repeat.

"We've worked together a long time, Danny, and never once in the last six years have you ever mentioned your father," he says.

His words pulse a new fear in my chest.

"And?" I ask.

"And he went to the media this morning letting them know that..." He pauses, and I freeze as a strange sensation rolls through me. It's overwhelming and terrifying as I wait for him to finish that sentence.

A PR crisis plus my father equals...

Fuck.

Did he go public with the tape?

"Let them know what?" I demand.

"Let them know how you've been mending your relationship with him, and you're getting closer and closer. It smelled like bullshit to me, but I wanted to check in with you first."

"Jesus Christ, Brad!" I yell at him. He scared the shit out of me that it was something really bad.

I mean...not that this is good, exactly, but it's not sex tape bad. It's not revealing my secret relationship with Alexis Bodega-level bad.

"I figured you wouldn't find it good, so I just wanted to check in if we need to do any damage control," he says.

"Fuck," I mutter.

"What?"

I debate what to tell him. I know he'd protect me, but he doesn't know the truth about Alexis and me, and I'm not ready to tackle that particular beast quite yet.

I decide to make it vague. "He's got some shit on me that could blow up not just my reputation but that of someone I care very much about."

"What's he got on you?" he asks.

My silence obviously speaks volumes.

He sighs. "I'll get in touch with Jodi," he says, naming my publicist.

"Thanks, Brad. And for now, let's just leave it be."

"You got it. I'm on call for you twenty-four-seven. Whenever you need it, man," he reminds me.

"I know. And I appreciate it." I end the call, knowing it won't be long before my mother sees this and starts asking questions.

I don't know if I can be vague with her the way I was with Brad, but she deserves the truth. I'm not exactly at liberty to discuss my sex life with my mother, though.

I decide to text Alexis.

Me: *My agent just called. I guess my dad is talking to the media about how we're getting closer. I'm worried about what he might do.*

My phone starts ringing before I hear back from her, and it's a Vegas number I don't recognize. I send the call to voicemail then head upstairs to shower.

When I get out, I have another handful of voicemails. I listen to the first one—a news agency in Vegas wanting the first comment about my situation with my father.

The others are all about the same thing. The news broke somewhere, and clearly it's everywhere.

I text Brad.

Me: *I'm getting media inquiries. Have Jodi write up a statement about how I'm not commenting at this time.*

On Deck

I eat breakfast with my nephews before we all hop in the car so I can go with her to drop them at school.

But as soon as they're out of the car, my mom glances over at me. She pulls into a parking spot in the lot and lets out a heavy sigh. "Are you going to tell me what's going on with your father?"

I tip my chin up as I keep my gaze out the window. "You saw?"

"It's everywhere, Danny. Of course I saw. And I know him, and I know you, and I know it's not true. So you can either tell me what's really going on, and I can help you find the answer, or you can sit in your silent misery the way you have been for the last twenty-four hours."

"My silent misery?" I ask, turning to look at her. "That's a little dramatic, don't you think?"

She shrugs. "Is it? You're clearly wrestling with some things, and if you don't want to talk about them, fine. That's your prerogative. But when you sulk around the house, you can't expect me not to check in, and when this news comes out about your father, well, you can't expect me to sit back and take it." Her voice is trembling with anger by the time she's done talking.

I sigh and keep my gaze focused out of the windshield. Cars come and go as they drop their little kids off at school, and honestly, a school parking lot is not where I figured I'd be having this conversation today. "He's blackmailing me." My voice comes out cold and flat.

"He's what?" she breathes.

I slide my head to the side on the headrest and look at her. I close my eyes for a beat and nod. "Blackmailing me. He planted a camera in my house, caught a private conversation and some other things between Alexis and me, and now he's using it to extort me for money."

"Oh my God, Danny," she breathes, sidestepping the *other things* he caught on camera. "That's horrible. I...I don't know what to say."

"It's bad enough that I've already paid him to keep quiet. But he also wants me to tell the world what a good father he is."

She makes a *pfft* sound, and I couldn't agree more.

"He's really something else," she says absently. "What are you going to do?"

I shrug. "No idea. Keep paying him to keep quiet? I feel like he went to the media to show me he isn't afraid to talk if I push him to it. Oh, and Rush has a private investigator cousin he's going to hook me up with to see what skeletons dear old Dad might be hiding in his closet."

"Are you sure you want to know?" she asks.

"You know, I really, really don't. But I also don't want to keep making payments when he doesn't deserve a cent of my money." I shrug.

"I don't blame you. Let me know how I can help."

I nod my thanks, and she starts navigating back toward my sister's place.

I wish there was something she could do to help, but for now, I think I have to wait to hear from Rush's cousin.

Chapter 26
Alexis

I clear the text message and slide my phone back into my pocket. I'll respond later when I'm not sitting beside my fiancé and across from my father and the wedding planner.

Rafe is showing us all the things that have been chosen for our wedding, and it feels...surreal.

I don't want any of this. I didn't ask for any of it, and these aren't the things I would have chosen for my wedding. Which sort of makes them perfect, really—so when I get married for *real* one day, I can pick all the things I ever wanted for my dream wedding. That way, they're not going to waste on this sham.

This is *somebody's* dream wedding, but it isn't *mine*.

"So we have the date and the venue. We'll have a small outdoor ceremony first followed by the reception. Most of the details are in place, but I need some names. Let's start with the best man, shall we?" Rafe looks over to Brooks.

Brooks looks up at my father, who's sitting next to Rafe. "Mr. Bodega, I'd be honored if you'd be my best man."

My father looks surprised. Shocked, even. But that melts away into approval. "I'd be honored." He turns to Rafe. "Can I still walk her down the aisle in that role?"

"Of course," Rafe says. "It'll be a little non-traditional, but it's your wedding."

I don't want my dad to walk me down the aisle. I want him to give me away when the wedding is *real*, but I can't exactly say that to him in front of Rafe, who believes it *is* real.

"I'd like to walk myself down," I say quietly.

Rafe looks at me and beams a little. "I love it. It's so trendy, and it'll be a springboard for women everywhere to talk about new traditions that represent women's rights." He turns to my father. "Thoughts?"

If my dad looked at Brooks with approval, he looks at me with disapproval. He opens his mouth to say something, but then he sighs. "Whatever Alexis wants."

"Maid of honor?" he asks, turning to me.

"I don't really have anyone in mind," I admit candidly. "I mentioned Leila to my dad, but I think I'd rather just not have one."

There's nobody I'd want to stand up with me believing in the sham when it's all a lie.

"Oh. My. God. Yes! No maid of honor. No escort down the aisle. Buck all the traditions, Alexis. Start your own trend. I *love* it." He holds both hands to his chest dramatically, and the drama of it all might be comedic if there was literally anything here worth laughing about other than the sham itself.

My dad's brows dip. "Won't that look strange if I'm his best man and she has no maid of honor?"

"No. You'll be the witness. Or, if you'd prefer, you could officiate."

On Deck

My dad's eyes light up a little. He *loves* being the center of attention, and he so rarely gets to be since he's usually the person creating opportunities for others to be in that role.

"What do you both think?" he asks Brooks and me.

"I agree wholeheartedly. I think that would be an even better role for you than best man," Brooks says. He turns to me. "Alexis?"

I nod. "It's fine." It's all fine. Everything's *fine*.

But none of it really *feels* all that fine.

"Right. We have our people, then. Anyone else? Flower girl, ring bearer, ushers?" he asks.

I glance at Brooks then shake my head.

I wish Danny could be there. I realize that makes absolutely zero sense, but if he could be an usher, I could talk to him before the wedding. He could tell me I'm doing the right thing.

It doesn't feel like the right thing.

And I know he'd never tell me it's the right thing.

I look up at my dad and see how happy this is making him.

That's the one thing I'm holding onto. He gets this merger. He can safely let go of the business and place it into Brooks's hands. It'll have the sort of future he wants it to have when he's no longer around to run it. It can stay in the family this way.

Gregory steps into the kitchen to get some coffee, and I know he's on my side. We haven't talked about it at all, but I can't help wondering what he thinks about all this.

He's on the inside, and if ever there was somebody I'd want by my side on my wedding day, it's him.

"Oh, what about Gregory as an usher?" I ask.

He freezes halfway across the kitchen.

"Gregory, would you be willing?" I press as I silently beg him with my eyes.

"Of course, ma'am." He nods at me and presses his lips together. "It would be my honor."

153

"Great, then," Rafe says, clapping his hands. He jots down something, and then he flips through his papers. "We've booked your morning beauty routine the day of, Alexis. You'll stay the night before at the ranch, and the stylists will begin on you bright and early. The evening before, we'll have a rehearsal dinner for close family and friends. The guest list numbers around three-fifty, and we'll need to pare that down to around a hundred, which is the max capacity at San Ysidro Ranch. We have photography, videography, and lighting booked. The cake is ordered. Stationery is ordered. In lieu of gifts, we've asked for donations to cancer research to honor your mother."

At least one good thing is coming from all this, I guess.

He continues down his checklist. "We have the bartender and liquor ready to go. Everything is chosen for the ceremony except rings, and we'll still need the script for the ceremony, including which poems or readings you prefer. But the décor, chairs, aisle runner, and transportation have all been handled. For the reception, I'll need your food and music preferences, but otherwise, I think we're all set." He slides a sheet of paper across the table toward us to review then glances up at Brooks. "And I'll need the honeymoon details, too."

"All the details?" Brooks deadpans, and I've never known him to be much of a funny guy.

Maybe that's one of the things I love so much about Danny. He can make me laugh with just a single look. I don't know if I've ever genuinely laughed with Brooks.

"Location, location, location," Rafe says. "And, of course, the *when*."

"We've not officially booked anything as of yet given Alexis's filming schedule," Brooks says. "But I have some dates and locations in mind."

"Care to share?" Rafe presses.

Brooks shakes his head. "I was planning to surprise my bride."

Surprise? Or kidnap me to a place nobody will know about? I keep that thought in my head.

"So romantic." Rafe looks at my would-be-husband with hearts in his eyes, and this is all just a smidge over the top for me when all I want to do is fly upstairs and call Danny back.

I haven't been able to. I've been locked in by my dad's side since he was released from the hospital last night, and Brooks is never very far away.

I'll escape at some point.

I need to see Danny. I need his arms around me. I need his lips on mine.

I need him to tell me everything is going to be okay.

Because the more time we spend apart, the more I fear it won't be.

Chapter 27
Danny

"Danny, hi, this is Chloe Ross. My cousin said you were looking into my services?"

"Hi Chloe, yes. I've got a, um...situation I need some help with," I say, glancing over at my mom. We just got back to my sister's house, and she's brewing us some coffee.

"Tell me a little about what's going on and what you're looking for me to do."

"My father is blackmailing me. He has a video from a camera he planted in my bedroom that has a very private conversation and other things on it that I wouldn't want to get out. I'd like to know if you can find anything on him that would allow me to get him to stop making threats."

"I assume you've ruled out turning him in to the police?" she asks.

"Correct. He'd have to turn over the tape, and there's some damning evidence on there I can't have getting out to anyone."

"Right. How much has he already taken from you?" she asks.

"A hundred grand plus the first hit to my reputation." I glance over as my mom's eyes widen at the dollar amount.

"I normally charge two-fifty an hour, but since you play with my cousin, it'll be two hundred. I'm estimating at least ten to twelve hours on this minimum. Will that be a problem?" she asks.

"I'll give you ten grand regardless of how many hours it takes as long as you find something."

"Oh, I'll find something. I'll shoot over a contract and a questionnaire for you to complete, and as soon as I get that back from you along with the deposit, I'll get started."

"I'll have it to you today."

"Excellent. I look forward to working with you. Oh, and Danny?" she adds, almost as an afterthought.

"Yeah?"

"Go Heat," she says warmly. "Congrats on an amazing season."

"Thanks, Chloe."

I cut the call, and a text comes through from her a few minutes later.

I answer the questions immediately, giving her all the information I have on my father so she can get started, and my mom watches me carefully as she sips her coffee.

Once I've sent her the contract back along with a ten percent deposit via Venmo, I glance up at my mom. "What?" I ask.

"Are you sure you're doing the right thing?" she asks.

"I'm sure." I nod resolutely. "How else am I supposed to battle this?"

"It's just…the last time you found something out about your father, the fallout was pretty bad. I don't want to see you go through that again." She nods pointedly at me.

"It's different this time," I say. I tap my finger on the table.

"How so?"

I clear my throat as I look up at her. "When I was seven, I caught my hero doing something terrible. The worst thing that'll happen this time is I'll catch the scum of the Earth doing something scummy."

She presses her lips together and reaches across the table to squeeze my hand. "I hope you find what you need, then."

"Me too."

I still haven't heard from Alexis, and I haven't heard from Chloe by the end of the day, either.

I'm not entirely sure if she got right to work on things or not, and I'm not sure what Alexis is up to, either. Luckily the boys are here to distract me, and my hotel room goes unused another night since nobody's meeting me there.

What a waste of money.

Leo wakes me up by breathing in my face again, and the boys head to school shortly after that. I find a new text from Alexis when I finally look at my phone. It was sent in the middle of the night.

Carrie: *Can't sleep without you. I'm sorry I've been quiet. My dad just got out of the hospital, and I've been his personal nurse. On top of the wedding plans between filming, I haven't been able to get away. I miss you. Are you still in California?*

I text her back even though she sent that one over five hours ago.

Me: *Yes. I'm still at my sister's place, and I still have that hotel in Long Beach. Any chance you can meet me there?*

Her response comes a couple of hours later, and this time, I'm blessed with a phone call.

"Hey," I answer.

"God, it feels good to hear your voice. Hi," she says.

"Hi. Are you okay?"

"Better now," she admits. "I'm so, so sorry. Things have just been bananas here. I'm on set right now, and this was literally the only moment I had free."

"Thanks for using it up on me."

"No one I'd rather use it up on."

"Same. Can you make it out to Long Beach?" I ask.

"I don't think I can make it work. Is there any chance you can swing by the set? I can have Gregory sneak you into my trailer, and we can..." She clears her throat. "Talk."

I laugh. "Talk. Right." I can practically see her blushing right now.

She giggles. "I love your laugh, and I love how you can make me laugh even when the world feels like it's crashing down on me."

"Hey, baby. We'll figure things out, okay? I promise."

"I'm holding you to that," she says. "Shit, I have to go, but I'll text you the address and what time to be here, okay?"

"I can't wait to see you," I admit.

"Same. Love you."

"I love you too," I say, but I think she has already hung up before hearing my words.

True to her word, a text comes through shortly after with the address and a time of five o'clock. I let my mom know I'll be heading to my hotel tonight, and she gives me a hug and tells me to take care of myself.

I tell her I will, but the truth is that I don't need to since I've got Alexis to take care of me.

It's a little over an hour to LA without traffic, but with traffic, it'll take close to two hours. So I hop in the car at three just to make sure I'm not late, and it's as I'm navigating toward the set that my phone rings, and I see it's Chloe calling.

"Hello?" I answer.

"It's Chloe Ross. I'm calling with an update."

On Deck

"What did you find?" I ask.

"I found a lot of things, but I think you're going to want to sit down for this."

"Well, I'm driving, so I am sitting," I say.

"You're sure?" she asks.

"Hit me with it."

"Your father is dying," she says.

"He's...he's what?" I ask, sure I heard her correctly, but I'm not sure why it doesn't hit me harder than it does. I should be upset about that, right? He's my father. He gave me life.

Except he abandoned me when I was seven, and he's been as good as dead to me since. He only shows up when he wants something, and this time it's money. The whole buying Olivia a graduation present was obviously a lie. He's setting his family up because he's about to kick the bucket, and he's using my money to do it.

"He has stage four lung cancer," she says, and her voice sounds far away for a beat. "He's got nothing left to lose, Danny. The doctors have given him less than a year."

"Oh." He was a smoker my entire childhood, and I remember him and my mother getting into fights about that when I was a kid. She wanted him to stop, and he didn't want to. I suppose there were other things he should have stopped that he also didn't bother with.

"I'm sorry to be the one to tell you that. I hope it's something that is useful to you," she says.

"No, no. Don't be sorry. It explains a lot. If he's got nothing left to lose, he might as well go out with a bang, right?" I say.

"I guess so. Want me to keep digging?" she asks.

"No, I think that's all I'll need. Thanks, Chloe. I'll send the rest of the payment by the close of business today."

"You don't have to. I didn't have to dig very hard to find this."

"You probably just saved me thousands of dollars, so it's the least I can do. Thanks again." I cut the call, not sure what else to say, and I sit with this news as I continue driving on toward Alexis.

Chapter 28
Alexis

I'm lucky enough to wrap my final scene for the day—for the year, actually, since we're going on hiatus until after the Christmas break to accommodate my wedding—at four-thirty, so I'm done earlier than I was expecting.

But my dad doesn't have to know that.

Gregory helps Danny sneak back to my trailer, and he shows up a little before five. I lift to a stand when the door opens, and I spot him with a baseball cap pulled down low over his eyes, and when he looks up and his eyes meet mine, I feel a sense of relief that he's here.

Except he looks…nervous. Stressed. Anxious. Something.

Sort of the way I'm feeling, I suppose.

He's twitchy as he makes his way toward me, and Gregory closes the door behind him as he seals us into privacy.

"What's wrong?" I ask immediately as I meet him halfway across the room.

"How'd you know?" he asks softly.

"Know what?"

"That something's wrong."

"It's all over you," I say, alarmed that he'd even ask that. "What is it?"

He clears his throat. "Don't be mad."

More alarm bells ring. "About what?"

"I told Cooper and Rush about the blackmail. And my mom."

I cover my face with my hands. "Oh my God, now your mom knows we're sleeping together."

"Babe, she probably put it together when you were there Thanksgiving weekend and we shared a bed," he says.

"Okay, I'm not mad, but why'd you tell everyone when you told me not to say a word?"

"My dad blabbed to the media this morning about how we're mending our relationship." He starts pacing around my small trailer rather than taking me into his arms. "I think it was his way of showing he's not backing down. He'll talk to the media if we push him to do it. That's why I told my mom, anyway—so she knew I wasn't genuinely getting close with that asshole again. And I told Rush and Cooper because I trust them and needed some advice because I feel like I'm handling everything wrong."

"You're not handling anything wrong, Danny," I say quietly. "This is uncharted for both of us."

"Yeah, it is. Rush thought I should see what I could find out about my dad to push back at him, and he gave me his private investigator cousin's info. Long story short, she found something on my dad." His eyes are down toward the ground, and then he glances up at me.

It's plain to see he's suffering here.

I'm just not sure why quite yet.

On Deck

"What did she find?" I whisper, a little nervous to hear the answer.

He clears his throat. "He's dying. He's got nothing to lose by blackmailing me for all I've got. And I'm not sure there's anything more dangerous than a man with nothing to lose."

"He's..."

"Dying," he repeats, and he's stone cold as he says the words. "Stage four lung cancer."

I walk toward him and wrap my arms around his waist. "Are you okay?"

"I, uh...I'm not sure," he admits as he holds me to him.

"Do you want to talk about it?" I ask.

He's quiet a beat, and I rest my head on his chest. His heart is beating steadily, and I think of how warm that heart is. How loving and giving. How kind and wonderful. This man is holding me in his arms after professing his love to me when I'm going to marry someone else. He's committed to waiting for me until we can start living our truth.

So whatever he's feeling, I need to be here to help him through it.

He rests his chin on top of my head, and when he speaks, his chest rumbles with the sound of his voice. "When you found out your dad was sick and in the emergency room, you ran to be with him. When I found out my dad is sick...I felt nothing. Or not even nothing, but worse, I had this sense that everything happens for a reason, and then I felt like I could use this news to get him to fucking stop what he's doing to me. What does that say about me?" His voice comes out pained, and I get the feeling that he feels worse about his reaction than he does about the actual news.

"It says you're perfectly normal, and you're entitled to feel absolutely however you feel," I say softly. I pull back a little to look up at him and lift to my tiptoes to press a kiss under his chin. "It says he's hurt you deeply, and you don't owe him a damn thing."

"Yeah, but shouldn't I want to help him?" he asks, and there's a hint of desperation there like he thinks he has to feel a certain way even though he doesn't. "Shouldn't I feel sad about it? He's my *father*, and instead of feeling bad about it, I don't. I just want him out of my life, and apparently, there's a surefire way that he'll be out of it within the next year."

"Oh, Danny," I say quietly. "If he had been there for you your entire life and was a good man who treated you the way a son should be treated, then you'd feel differently. But he wasn't. He did terrible things to your mom, to you, to your sister, and now to me. Nobody would judge you for feeling any type of way about him after all he's put you through."

"Thank you," he says, dropping his lips to mine for a beat. "I just keep wondering how I can use it to get him to back off of us."

"What are you thinking?" I ask. I pull out of his arms to allow him to resume his pacing. I head over to the couch and sit as I watch him.

He presses his lips together. "I'm not sure yet. I think he's probably after my money to set his family up once he's gone. He made up some dumb story and chose to blackmail me rather than making amends and just fucking asking for it, so that tells you the type of person we're dealing with. I guess I could offer to pay off his debts in exchange for him erasing that tape. I just…I still feel like he could do a lot of damage with the time he has left, and he doesn't care if it lands him in prison or whatever because he's going to die soon anyway."

"God, what a horrible way to live out the final days of your life," I murmur.

"Yeah. But it's what he has chosen." He sighs. "What do *you* think I should do with it?"

"Does his family know?" I ask.

"That he's sick?" he asks, and I nod. He shrugs. "No idea."

"If they don't, then you know one of his secrets that he doesn't want getting out just like we don't want that tape getting out."

He nods. "It just...it feels so wrong to use his illness against him."

"More wrong than planting a video recording device in his son's bedroom and catching him banging his secret girlfriend?" I point out.

"Touche," he says. "What do you think about getting Gregory's opinion on the whole thing?"

I wrinkle my nose. "I mean, on the one hand, it would be like admitting to my own father I'm banging the bad boy of baseball. On the other hand...I think he already knows."

"He definitely already knows." He offers a little chuckle, and I laugh, too, before I grab my phone and shoot a text to Gregory asking him to come on in.

Gregory raps twice at the door before I head over to open it, and he slips inside.

"Ma'am?" he asks, looking between Danny and me.

"We have a little, uh..." I glance over at Danny. "A situation."

"A situation?" he asks.

"My estranged father planted a video recorder in my bedroom," Danny begins. "I didn't know, and he caught a private conversation between Alexis and me that's quite damning along with...other activities."

Gregory clears his throat, and I blush profusely, the heat curling around my neck. "And he's using it for..."

"Money," Danny says. "He's already taken a hundred grand with his blackmail to take the tape public, and a friend suggested

I hire a private investigator to look into what secrets he's hiding that I can hold over him."

"And what turned up?" he asks.

"How do you know I hired the PI?" Danny asks.

Gregory gives him a look. "I wasn't born yesterday, Mr. Brewer. Of course you took the shot. Now tell me what you found out so I can take action."

"Take action?" Danny repeats. "What are you, MacGyver?"

"No, sir. I'm a private security guard for the most famous pop singer in the world, and my job is to disarm any potential threats to my client. This is a threat."

Danny draws in a heavy breath. "Stage four lung cancer. He's got nothing left to lose."

Gregory nods once. "Would you like me to take care of this for you?"

"How?" Danny asks.

Gregory's eyes dart quickly between us. "Do you really want to know?"

"When he asks that, the answer is usually no," I say dryly.

Danny purses his lips for a beat in thought. "I'll handle it myself."

"The offer is on the table should you want to take it," he says.

"I appreciate that, Gregory. And all you do for Alexis, too. More than I can ever say."

My chest warms at his words, and Gregory politely nods.

"Gregory?" I say, and he turns to look at me. "I'd like to stay the night with Danny at his hotel."

"What about your father, ma'am?" he asks.

"Make something up. I don't care what it is."

He nods again, and I'm thankful for his discretion and protection.

"I'll follow you there and stay at the same hotel, and I'll take care of your father," he says.

On Deck

I shoot him a grateful look, and then I turn to Danny. "Ready?"

He nods, and I pull my hoodie up, put on my sunglasses, and follow Gregory outside, where he helps me duck discreetly into Danny's car.

And then we make the trip toward his hotel in Long Beach, his hand on my leg as we taste the first bite of freedom we've had in far too long.

Chapter 29
Danny

My hand hasn't left her leg in the twenty minutes we've been driving back toward my hotel, and her hand hasn't left the top of mine.

"Can I tell you something?" she asks.

I glance over at her as I flex my fingers over her thigh. "Anything, anytime, anywhere."

She gives me a thoughtful look at my words. "I like that. But this is something that's been weighing kind of heavy on me, and I feel like I need to say it."

My brows crinkle as I brace myself for something. The end, maybe. She's telling me she's out. She's marrying Brooks. She wants to be with him. She doesn't want to deal with this bullshit from my father. It's not worth it to her.

My mind races with all the negative possibilities.

"That picture of you and that girl from the bar..." she begins. She draws in a breath. "I wanted you to know that it hurt to see you with someone else, and I don't want to be one of those couples who falls into silly miscommunication traps, so I just had to say the words. I felt hurt even though I know it's so hypocritical of me to say that given that I'm *marrying* another man, but for a minute, I thought maybe you didn't want to bother with me anymore, that this whole thing with Brooks and my dad and the wedding is overwhelming, that you wanted to run as far away as you could, and maybe I wouldn't blame you for that."

My chest tightens that she's having the exact same sort of fears that I'm having.

"Lex," I say softly. "I'm not running, okay? I'm not running." I say it twice so she really hears it.

"I think maybe it's part of why I didn't call you back. I mean, I couldn't. My dad was always in the room, and I had to make sure he was okay. But I maybe could have texted, and I didn't. I retreated a little because I got scared." She's baring her soul to me, and the thought of it all is overwhelming.

It pulses a new feeling inside me that's both terrifying and beautiful. It's more than love.

It's home.

"It's okay. I get it. And to be perfectly honest, the *what if* ran through my mind. What if I took her or someone else up on the offer?"

Her head whips to my profile at my pause. "Why didn't you?"

"Ultimately what it came down to is that not a single one of them has ever made me feel the way you do. And *that* is what I'm addicted to. It's what I've fallen for. It's why I keep showing up for you even though you're marrying somebody else. It's you, Alexis. Only you. And there may be no guarantees, but I don't care. I'm here anyway."

She quietly swipes at her cheeks at my words, and I squeeze her thigh.

On Deck

"It's only you for me, too, Danny. I promise you." There's a hint of begging in her tone, as if she's begging me to believe her.

And I do believe her. I believe in us. I *trust* in us. And I trust that she'll handle my heart carefully. It should be scary considering I've never given it to someone else to hold, but it's not. It can't be scary when it's so damn right.

We arrive at the hotel. I usher her in through a side entrance, and we take a service elevator up to the penthouse floor where my room is located.

Nobody spotted us going in, and now we have some actual *time* together.

She glances around the suite and moves toward the window with a water view. "So beautiful," she says softly.

I walk toward her and wrap one arm around her waist from behind. I lift her hair to the side so I can press my lips to her neck, and she moans a little as she leans back into me, her gaze still out on the beach. But then she spins in my arms and reaches up to pull my head down to hers, and she initiates a kiss that begins urgent and leads me exactly where we both want to go. Where we both *need* to go.

I pull her closer to me as she wraps her arms around me, our bodies already swaying with the lust that's always present between us as my need for her rushes straight to my cock. I push my hips toward hers, and she moans when she feels how ready I am for her.

It's been too long without this connection, and I'm aching for her.

Her hand trails down until she's palming my cock over my jeans, and I run my hands down her torso until I find the hem of her dress. I pull it up and over her head so she's standing in front of me in just her bra and panties, and I've never seen such a gorgeous sight in my whole life.

I stare at her, and then I grab her into my arms and toss her down on the bed. I climb up so I'm hovering over her, and I let my hips drag down toward hers so she can feel my length against her pussy, the only separation between us my jeans and her panties.

"We're both still wearing far too many clothes," she says as my lips graze her neck, and I have to agree with the woman. She's right.

I stand and strip naked in two seconds flat.

As I've said, it's been too long.

I reach for her panties and yank them down her legs while she unhooks her bra, and I climb back on top of her. I fist my cock and tease her clit with the head of it. I feel her wet warmth as she's so goddamn ready for me, and I want so badly to push into her, but I know the sooner it starts, the sooner it ends. So instead, I pull my hips back out of reach and stop teasing her for a beat, instead dragging my lips down her neck and to her breast.

I suck her nipple into my mouth as I reach over and pinch the other one between my finger and my thumb, and she lets out a soft cry at the feel. I bare my teeth against her nipple, and I'm rewarded with a moan. I take my time on her tits, lavishing one with my mouth as I massage the other with my hand, and then I move back up to kiss her some more.

I tease her with my cock again, thrusting against her clit to her begging moans, and eventually I dip into her just the slightest bit because I can't take the anticipation building between us any longer.

"Oh God," she moans as her body trembles beneath mine, and I hold still with just the tip inside her.

It takes every fiber of my power not to thrust all the way in, especially when she digs her heels into my ass to urge me in.

I hold steady even though it kills me.

"God, Danny, please. Please," she groans.

On Deck

"Please what?" I ask her. My eyes are on her, and her eyes are closed.

"Go deeper." She's begging, and it's hot as fuck.

"Open your eyes and tell me what you want," I demand.

Her eyes fly open, and they're flashing when they meet mine. "Just fuck me already!" she yells at me, and now I'm sensing some anger, and holy fuck, it does what it needs to do.

I slam into her, and her eyes roll back as she clutches onto the sheets.

"Oh God, oh God, oh God!" she cries as I drive into her over and over, picking up speed as I *just fuck her already* as requested.

My thrusts are downright chaotic and messy as I pump hard and quick strokes into her, and I feel myself getting too close too fast.

I pull out of her to give myself a minute.

She's panting as she glares up at me. "Don't stop now!" she screams.

"I'm going to come all over your tight cunt if I don't take a second," I admit.

"Then do it. Give all that come to my cunt," she murmurs, and holy fucking shit, have hotter words ever been spoken? I've never heard her use the word *cunt* before, and somehow hearing Alexis Bodega tell me to give her all my come nearly makes me spill all over her tits.

But she wants it in her cunt, so I shove back into her and slow my drives down to deep, long strokes.

"Oh my God!" she screams. "Danny, yes, yes, yes!"

I hold myself steady inside her for a beat before I draw back, and then I slam hard into her again. It takes me three more strokes before the fire builds up my spine and I start to come inside her. I hold still as my eyes find hers, an intimacy passing between us that's stronger than anything I've ever felt before. I spill into her, her cunt feeding on my come as if she needs it for her very survival, and her face twists with pleasure.

"I'm coming," she cries in a whisper, and her pussy clenches onto me as I ride out my climax. She lets go of the sheets she's been clutching as she wraps her arms around me, her fingernails digging into the skin of my back as she gives into the pleasure.

I watch her face through the whole thing, and I don't know if I've ever seen anything so beautiful as making the woman I love come like that.

I collapse on top of her as we both come down from the wave, the afterglow stepping into place as I slip out of her.

I shift to her side so I'm not crushing her, and I think we both might fall asleep for a bit.

It's nice, this moment—being here together without worrying what else is going on, that there's a wedding in the works taking place far too soon, being free to just be ourselves together. Not worrying that there's a camera planted somewhere in here catching our intimate moments.

Eventually I force myself up out of bed, and I clean off my cock before I put some clothes on. She gets up, too, and she heads to the bathroom. I lay her clothes out on the bed for her, and she picks them up when she returns while I stand by the window gazing out at the water.

"Should we order something for dinner?" she asks while she hooks her bra.

I nod. "Probably." I think about what I want to say to her. There's a lot to say, and also…there's nothing to say.

Now that we've had that moment together, I fear how long it'll be before we can escape to do this again.

The media will be keeping a close watch over her as her wedding date looms closer and closer. It was risky bringing her here today, and we only managed it with Gregory's help.

On Deck

It will just get harder and riskier from here, and I'm not sure what we're supposed to do about that.

I open my mouth to say something—I'm not sure what—but she beats me to it.

"Danny, I don't know what to do. I want to be with you. I don't want to marry Brooks."

"Then marry me," I murmur.

The words are out before I can stop them.

"What?" she breathes.

"Marry me. Be with me."

She stares at me.

"It'll solve all our problems. You can't marry Brooks if you're already married to me."

"*What?*" she repeats. "I...I can't. We're *days* away from the wedding, Danny. I have to do this. I have to marry him."

"You don't have to, Lex" I whisper.

I just hope my words are convincing enough.

Chapter 30
Alexis

I clench my fists at my side as I gear up for a fight. Danny and I haven't gotten into a fight yet. It's been magic. Bliss. Mutual understanding. It's probably the healthiest relationship I've ever been in...you know, except for the whole *secret* aspect.

All couples fight. Bickering, arguing—it's just part of life.

But this...this is striking me from out of left field.

I can't just *marry* him. I'm set to marry Brooks. I have a small engagement party tomorrow evening after I film all morning and I shouldn't even be *here* right now with Danny but I had the burning need to be there for him after what he found out about his father.

His words to *marry* him pulse an anger in me that's a little scary.

"I don't *have* to? Yes, Danny. Yes, I do. I don't *want* to, but I agreed to it, and my dad has me backed into a corner. If I want my masters and control over my career, I have to do this."

"You just said you don't want to. If you don't want to…then don't," he says.

"It's not that simple!" I yell.

"That's what he's making you think, Alexis. Have you had a lawyer look over your contract? One of your own, I mean—not one your father hired."

I press my lips together.

The truth is that I've *thought* about doing that, but I haven't. And I don't even have a solid reason why I haven't. I guess because I thought I could trust my dad.

Maybe Danny is right…but maybe I am, and I'm not sure how to find the answer to that.

"I'll take your silence as your answer. Let *me* look over it, then. Stop letting him emotionally manipulate you," he says.

"My father isn't the same as your father," I hiss, and I regret the words as soon as they're out of my mouth.

He's dealing with a lot, and of course he already knows that. I don't need to pile on top of him by pointing it out.

"I know that," he says quietly—ominously, almost. "Mine is blackmailing us. Yours is ruining us. Which is worse?"

I press my lips together as I feel the sting of tears behind my eyes. Maybe he's hurt that I rejected his proposal, so he's lashing out.

Or maybe he's exactly right and I'm just too close to the situation to realize it.

Rather than respond to his words, I say, "I don't want to fight with you when this very well could be the last time we see each other before I marry Brooks."

He averts his gaze out the window and lets out a heavy sigh. "You're right. I don't want to fight, either. This is just…a lot."

"I know it is. And you know where my heart is."

"Yeah. I do. But I also have to watch you marry that douchebag and trust that your father is going to let you unwind this mess in the end."

"I have to trust in that, too. And we have paperwork being drafted that will ensure it," I say.

He nods. "Paperwork. Right. Look, Brooks is a smart guy. What makes you think he will just give up and let you go in the end?"

He's got a point. It's something that's been in the back of my mind the whole time, but I know Brooks. He wouldn't take advantage of the situation, and I don't know exactly what he's getting out of the deal, but I have faith that my dad will make sure he gets whatever's coming to him.

"It's something to think about, I guess. But I feel like you're bringing all this up at the eleventh hour, Danny. I'm committed. I have a dress. The wedding planner has finalized all the details. The guest list is complete. The media has been tipped off. It's a train barreling down the tracks, and I am powerless to stop it at this point," I say.

He takes a step toward me, and then another. "I have your solution, Lex." He pulls me into his arms. "Marry me. Run away from it all. Fuck the wedding planner and the dress and the details. It's just money. It's not *this*." He presses his lips to mine.

It's tempting, but there's the whole issue of my agent and my masters.

As if he could read my mind, he says, "We'll figure out together how you can take control of your career. I've seen it done before. You don't need him. There are loopholes. You can re-record your albums and release your AVs."

"AVs?"

"Alexis's Version," he clarifies.

I close my eyes. "I just...I can't, Danny." I pull out of his arms and push him away, the symbolism not lost on me that as

I'm physically pushing him away, the emotional divide between us is also widening. "Please stop forcing the issue because you already know what I want, and I can't have it, and it's tearing me up inside."

He nods. "Okay. I'll stop. But the offer is on the table, and I'm not rescinding it. Now what do you want me to order for dinner?"

We put the focus on what to order for a bit, but the conversation is still there in the background, simmering away.

After we eat, we lay in bed together.

"When do you have to go back to Vegas?" I ask.

"I have a charity event in a couple of days. I figured I'd spend one more day with my mom and the boys and then head back," he says.

"Will you be here next weekend?" I hear the begging in my tone, and as screwed up as it sounds, I don't know if I can make it down the aisle toward Brooks if Danny isn't close by.

I'm fighting for us by marrying the wrong man. I know that sounds crazy, and it even does in my own head, but I'm taking control of my life.

This is the only way I see how to do that.

I just hope we can escape to the other side unscathed.

Chapter 31
Alexis

Gregory covered with a bachelorette party that was a total fabrication, but my dad somehow bought it.

While I want the next week to slow down, it seems like time speeds up. My dad fills my every waking moment with wedding details.

Photo shoots.

Small engagement parties with various groups of well-known celebrity guests.

Vendor meetings.

Sales pitches.

Instagram ready content.

More photo shoots.

Fake smiles I'm trying my hardest to pass off as real.

He's covering all the bases. It's exhausting, and I barely have time to get in touch with Danny as we get closer and closer to the big day. He left for Vegas a couple of days ago, and I'm not sure what he decided about his dad because we haven't had enough time to talk about it. But news hasn't yet broken about our secret affair, so I'm banking on the fact that Danny is somehow keeping him quiet.

We only have one more day that we need him to stay quiet before the wedding.

If he comes out with our tape after that, at least the wedding will be over. It'll sound like old news from a scorned old man— or something along those lines.

I keep telling myself that, anyway, because the alternative of him actually giving that tape to the media is scarier than I'd like to admit even to myself.

I wish I could see it. I wish I could know how clear my face is, whether it's obvious that it's really me and not just some lookalike. Apart from the World Series "Kiss Seen Around the World," Danny and I have never been linked together publicly— even though we've done our fair share of linking privately.

Maybe Gregory knows what Danny decided about his father, but I haven't had much chance to chat privately with him this week, either. I'm sandwiched between my father and Brooks pretty much everywhere we go. I feel like a prisoner in my own home more than ever.

I think they're purposely not letting me out of their sight because they're afraid of what I might do if I get out.

They're afraid I'll run.

I can't pretend like Danny's words haven't played on repeat in my brain since he said them.

"Marry me."

Marry me.

Was he serious?

And…what if I did?

What if I ran out on this wedding? What would my dad do, really?

On Deck

I'm sure he'd find a way to make it happen anyway. He'd rope me into the wedding I never wanted so he could get his damn merger.

I keep thinking there's no other way out of this, but what if there is?

What if Danny's right?

What if the merger could still happen without me marrying Brooks?

He said it would make it easier. He said it would help the merger go through quickly. He didn't say it wouldn't happen without this piece.

Danny's words repeat while I sit at yet another engagement party with some of my father's business associates.

Marry me. Be with me.

It'll solve all our problems. You can't marry Brooks if you're already married to me.

He's right.

And the more I think about it...the more I want it.

But I can't just duck out on all this now.

And so I smile as some designer helps me into a dress to wear to our rehearsal at the ranch the night before the wedding.

Marry me. Be with me.

I play off the tears as happy ones while I walk down the aisle toward Brooks at the rehearsal, a few close business associates and family members gathered with us, everyone keeping their eyes on my every move.

Marry me. Be with me.

I force a fake smile as my father looks proudly down at us as our officiant. He gives us a quick summary of the order of events, and then we're free to go to our dinner.

Marry me. Be with me.

His words play more heavily as the clock ticks on toward the day of the wedding, and as morning dawns after a restless night, I check my text messages.

I have one from Danny sent late last night after I must have gone to bed.

DJ: *I'm at the Ritz in Santa Barbara, building 9, room 26. I'm here and close. Tell me what I can do to help you.*

I stare at his text.

Tell me what I can do to help you.

I don't have a text waiting for me from my future husband.

We parted ways last night without so much as a kiss, but I didn't kiss my father, either. My father stayed the night in the same three-bedroom suite as me, presumably to ensure I didn't run out on this whole nightmare.

I'm not going to run, though I have to say, the text from Danny this morning makes me want to.

I don't want to reply back this early and wake him, so I take a quick shower first.

When I get out, I have another text from him. I pull on the fluffy white bathrobe as I read his words.

DJ: *I'm awake and thinking about you. I wish I could talk to you. I wish I could say the things I need to say. Things like don't do this. Things like I love you. Things like I was serious when I said you should marry me instead. I know I'm risking a lot by texting this to you, but I'm desperate. We can't waste a year or two or even another fucking minute. Don't marry him. Marry me.*

I stare at his words as tears heat behind my eyes.

I hear a knock at the door.

In a fit of panic, I delete the message.

It doesn't matter.

I don't need that text.

I memorized the beautiful sentiment the moment I read the words. They're engraved on my heart forever.

On Deck

"Alexis? You okay in there?" It's my dad.

"I'm okay! Just got out of the shower!"

"I've ordered some breakfast for you. Should be here any moment. Happy wedding day, my darling girl," he says.

I can't help when the tears start their freefall.

This is wrong. All wrong. *So* wrong.

And yet, I float through the motions anyway.

I don't bother with my hair and make-up since a crew is coming up shortly to do it all for me.

I don't bother with much of anything, really. I'm not hungry enough to eat, so I pick at the egg white veggie omelet my dad ordered for me.

"I have the final prenuptial agreement," he says. He pushes some papers over toward me. "It's fairly basic and protects your assets should you decide to seek dissolution."

I should read it. I know I should…and so I do.

But my frame of mind isn't what it should be right now.

I flip through it and see the words but don't really comprehend them.

It says *whereas* a bunch of times and something about marital assets, separate assets, debts, and spousal support.

It looks pretty standard to me, yet the pen is poised in my hand as I contemplate what to do.

I have to sign it. I have to get this lie underway.

My father encourages me gently to try to eat, attributing my behavior to nerves…not to heartbreak.

But that's what this is.

Pure and simple.

There are no guarantees that Danny is going to stick around and see this through with me. I hope he does. I pray he does. But I wouldn't blame him if he didn't.

There's a lot at stake and a lot for us both to lose...particularly given his past and the very values he holds dear.

I sign the paper.

There's a knock at the door.

My father answers it and returns with a box. He opens it first to ensure it's safe, and then he hands it over to me with a crinkled brow of curiosity. "There's no note. Who's it from?"

I look inside the box to find a single chocolate long john and an order of crispy bacon.

My chest feels heavy as I stare at the food.

I close my eyes as I lie to my father. "I have no idea."

"Then you shouldn't eat it." He pulls the box out of my reach, and it feels so symbolic as he keeps finding ways to pull me further and further away from Danny.

The stylists descend.

I start with a massage for relaxation. I'm too tense, they tell me.

I have a manicure and pedicure.

I get my make-up done.

My hair.

I slip into the dress.

I don't feel anything.

I haven't written Danny back.

I don't know if I can. I don't know what to say.

I'm sorry.

I smile for the photos before the ceremony.

It's not real.

I wish I had a friend here to talk me out of this.

I wish I had a friend here to tell me I'm doing the right thing.

I wish I had a friend.

"It's time," my father says to me.

I nod.

On Deck

"I'll see you up there," he says. He moves to stand in front of me. "I love you, honey. Thank you for doing this. You're doing the right thing, and I promise, it'll be a year at most, and maybe you'll even change your mind about Brooks by then."

Change my mind?

Change my mind?

I haven't changed my mind in the four years I've been *seeing* him. I'm not going to in the next year, either.

I offer a small smile and a nod, emitting no clues about how I'm really feeling here—like I'm dangling off the edge of a cliff and there's nobody there at the bottom to catch me.

Except there is.

Danny is waiting at the bottom to hold me in his arms.

My father hugs me one last time before he heads out of the bridal suite so he can take his place at the front of the stage to officiate this sham.

I'm alone for a minute.

And it's one minute that has the power to change everything. *Everything.*

I have a man twenty minutes away who loves me for me and wants to marry me because he loves me. I have a man in the suite next to mine who wants to marry me for a business transaction.

So why am I marrying the wrong one?

I only get one life.

I signed it away when I was sixteen.

I likely signed more of it away when I carelessly signed those papers this morning.

Why am I continuing to let my dad control it for me?

I stare at myself in the mirror.

I didn't choose this dress, or this hairstyle, or the crown atop my head. I didn't choose the flowers or the location.

And I certainly didn't choose the groom.

There's a knock at the door, and I draw in a deep breath before I head over to open it.

Gregory stands there.

"Ms. Bodega. A lovely sight to behold as always." He nods cordially at me, and I just stand there staring a bit dumbfounded at him.

"It's time, ma'am." His words are meant to nudge me.

I step out of the bridal suite into the empty hallway.

I look to my left.

Just beyond that door, all the guests are seated.

The groom is waiting for me. My father is waiting for me.

I look to my right.

Out that door is a vehicle that the man in front of me holds the keys to, and that vehicle could take me just twenty short minutes away straight to the man I love.

Straight to the man who has been waiting to hear from me since early this morning.

Straight to the man I want to be with.

I look left again and right again.

"Alexis?" Gregory says, prompting me again. "You have to go."

My eyes fix on one door as I make a choice.

I press my lips together and nod.

TO BE CONTINUED IN BOOK 4, BASES LOADED

Alexis is backed into a corner as she looks between two doors. Behind door number one is the man her father is pushing her to marry, the man who's good for her brand and her future. Behind door number two is me: the bad boy of baseball who happens to be the man she has fallen in love with.

I wish we could just run away together. I promised I'd wait for her no matter how long it took. I'd wait forever if I had to. She's worth it.

But the bases are loaded, and as we run toward the final out, we have no idea what's waiting on the other side.

Acknowledgments

I'll save my acknowledgments for the final book! I can't wait for you to see what's coming next...

xoxo,
Lisa Suzanne

About the Author

Lisa Suzanne is an Amazon Top Ten Bestselling author of swoon-worthy superstar heroes, emotional roller coasters, and all the angst. She resides in Arizona with her husband and two kids. When she's not chasing her kids, she can be found working on her latest romance book or watching reruns of *Friends*.

Also by Lisa Suzanne

HOME GAME

Vegas Aces Book One
#1 Bestselling Sports Romance

CURVEBALL

Vegas Heat: The Expansion Team
Book One

Made in United States
Orlando, FL
08 April 2024